BIG DOGS
with Little Tales

Stories by: Clint Heverly

Original art by: Liz Walk, Connie Coyne

And

Denise Eileen Thurman

ISBN: 1451546211
ISBN-9781451546217

Dedication

This book is dedicated to enthusiastic educators everywhere, especially to the extraordinary few we recall with great fondness. They were the instructors who made their lessons engaging, encouraged life-long learning, and taught us to believe in ourselves – all with grace, humility and humor.

Special thanks to the following teachers who had the greatest impact on the author and artists of this book. May their names live forever!

- Earl Barnhart
- Richard Dean
- Jean Fortney
- Benson Noyce
- Jane McFann
- Stuart Frost
- Elizabeth Foley
- Mrs. Bogardes
- Diane Van Deusen
- Rheyna Laney
- Mathew J. James
- Thomas Jacobson
- Mr. Tatro
- Dorothy Gade
- Candace Birchfield

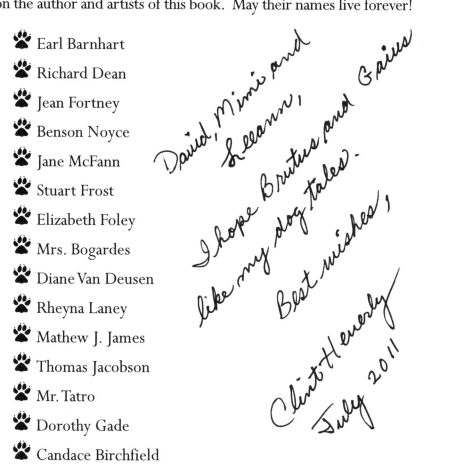

David, Mimi and Leeann,
I hope Brutus and Gaius like my dog tales -
Best wishes,
Clint Heverly
July 2011

Every Dog
Has His Day

Story by **Clint Heverly**

Portrait by **Elizabeth Walk**

FRANKLIN HEVERLY
Leader of the Pack

Some tales are make—believe and some tales have actually happened. You can rest assured, dear reader, that everything in this tale is true — whether it happened or not.

Who hasn't dreamt of performing a noble deed and hoped for a moment of glory? 'Hope' is a tiny word, but for those who dare to hope, any grand dream is possible. And so it was for a dog, named Franklin, who suffered so greatly that hope was often all he had.

Not so long ago, a Chocolate Labrador retriever, named Franklin, lay on his stomach, chin on paws, facing down the lane from his master's house atop Moore Hill. In a nearby pen were more dogs, the sled dogs of the master. Their names were Nilla, Lola, Oreo, Tiny, Ajax, Barky and Hatcher. They were Franklin's best dog buddies, now. But there was a time when Franklin thought he'd sooner be dead than be near these dogs — or any dogs, for that matter!

As Franklin stared down the lane, his half-awake mind recalled the odd events that brought him to this place in life; a place where he no longer suffered, a place that now felt good. But his daydreams were suddenly interrupted when the sled dogs sent up a chorus of warning barks. Franklin came to his senses and was greeted by yips and yelps and the vision of several puppies galloping up the hill toward him. "Is that him? Is that Franklin, the hero of Moore Hill?" one approaching youngster cried out.

The pups slowed to a trot and then to a deferential walk, and Franklin heard another say, "Oh, that's him, alright. I saw him outside the Dirty Dawg Saloon a while back. The Flatlanders claim he's a one-dog wrecking crew!"

Franklin wanted to take satisfaction from their words of praise, but he couldn't. For, you see, he had been mercilessly ridiculed recently by every canine he encountered – even by his pals in the nearby dog pen. Those painful memories worked to check his pride as he greeted the young dogs.

"What brings you whelps to Moore Hill?" asked Franklin, with a welcoming smile on his face.

Being in the presence of their first honest-to-goodness hero, the puppies were, at first, too awe-struck to speak. Eventually, though, a stubby-tailed beagle worked up his courage and dared to ask, "We want to know if it's fact, Franklin. We want to hear about the Wompus. They say you know all about 'em. They say you're a hero for fightin' 'em off! Please tell us your story. Won't 'cha? Huh? Huh? Won't 'cha? Won't 'cha?"

Heeding the little dog's request, Franklin wet his lips, took a deep breath and began his unusual tale.

"I don't know about this hero stuff, but I do know about the Wompus. Why, I was about your age when I first heard of the creature, the foulest beast known to dogdom. As my mates and I played among a group of elders one day, an Irish setter barked out, 'Ol' Jack, here, is a bona fide hero! Yup, yup; H-E-R-O! Ah-huh! Ah-huh! Ya put the chase to the Wompus last night; put the fear of God into that devil, didn't ya, Jackie boy?'"

Just hearing him say "Wompus" made Franklin's young visitors gasp and shiver. Nevertheless, they begged to hear more, so the big Lab continued.

"Ol' Jack, a stout-looking hound of no particular pedigree, then told the spookiest story I ever heard. He said he was feeling no pain as he headed home from the Dirty Dawg Saloon the previous night when, all of a sudden, he picked up the most disgusting scent imaginable. 'It was an odor so sickening,' said Jack, 'it would make cat poop smell like filet mignon!'"

"Ol' Jack soon realized he'd wandered into big trouble, for he spotted a god-awful critter, down on all fours, just a few feet in front of him. Besides being smelly, it was hairy and dirty and its eyes shone an evil red in the moonlight. 'It was the size of two St. Bernards,' recalled Jack, 'and uglier than Satan himself!'"

"As the stinky thing snuffled the ground, it began to mumble, mumble about being so hungry it could eat a dog. 'I smells me a dog,' said the Wompus, 'I know he's here. When I finds 'im, I'll scrunch 'im, I'll munch 'im and I'll eat 'im all up!'"

"'Hearing that threat,' confessed Jack, 'made my spittle run dry, my tail tuck beneath my tummy and my bladder empty without lifting a leg! To be honest, mates, all I could do was bark bloody murder and the Wompus – for that's what the old-timers say it was – took off like a cat outta Hell. If that makes me a hero, then I guess I am. Every dog has his day. Yessiree, every dog has his day.'"

"After he finished his account of the Wompus, we showed ol' Jack such great respect and admiration that I swore to perform a glorious deed someday, so that I, too, would be seen as a hero – just like Jack! But little did I suspect that my dream of fame and glory would be replaced by a daily struggle for survival!"

Their mouths agape, their tongues panting from excitement, but otherwise not moving a muscle, the puppies listened intently as Franklin picked up his story.

"Shortly after hearing Jack's Wompus tale, I was sold to a human family who neglected me. Oh, all dogs know the story. You're given as a gift to a child who says you're the prettiest puppy in the whole world; a child who promises to feed and water you, play with you, clean up after you and, of course, love you forever. But not being taught responsibility themselves, children soon forget their responsibility to you. And that led to my first test in life."

"I was chained outside and virtually forgotten. Often hungry, thirsty and yearning to be loved, I was, instead, teased and tormented by the children and kicked and beaten by the adults. I was living the nightmare all dogs fear!"

"But through it all, one thing gave me hope. It was something ol' Jack said in his Wompus story: 'Every dog has his day,' advised Jack. 'Every dog has his day.' Well, I knew I'd never had my day, so I figured I had one coming. When times were bad – and that was most of the time – I silently chanted my mantra to give me strength. 'Every dog has his day. Every dog has his day.'"

"But as I grew older, life became bleaker, for I became weaker and more depressed. And as I got bigger, no one even cared enough to adjust my collar, so it actually grew into my neck – it caused such an awful soreness! Nevertheless, I fought through the pain of those dark hours, all with the power I got from Jack's words of hope. 'Every dog has his day. Every dog has his day.'"

Franklin halted his tale of woe at this point, for he noticed that all of the youngsters were sobbing. So, he moved among them – patting their shoulders, scratching their heads, wiping away their tears – and finally restored calm. Then, at their urging, he resumed his heartbreaking account.

"When I was feeling as low as low could be – and starting to doubt that I'd ever have my day – a true miracle happened! Master John and Mistress Carol, owners of that house you see over yonder, rescued me from a life of misery. They brought me here and nursed me to health. They showed me how to love and trust again. They trained me to obey; trained me to be a good dog. Now a member of their pack, I went where they went, lived where they lived and I was even treated to ice cream at the end of each day – life was good!"

"I was a fortunate dog, now; fortunate enough to be having my day. However, I feel it's my duty to warn you pups about fortune, for fortune is a fickle thing. You can be a lucky dog one day, then a dog in despair the next."

Tilting their heads from side to side in a quizzical manner, Franklin's youthful audience showed great confusion. "How could good fortune turn sour so quickly?" they wondered. Sensing their bewilderment, but also a desire to hear more, Franklin returned to his saga.

"The next part of my story will not be one of physical suffering like I just described. No, young'ins, it'll be a tale of emotional torment, instead. Unfortunately, I can testify that one's just as bad as the other. Here's what happened to me next, right over there in Master John's house."

"It was the Dog Days of summer, a few years back, and the household had been fast asleep for quite awhile. But as I snoozed by the kitchen door, I was rudely awakened by a terrible stench, and it was coming from a creature atop a nearby counter. Large, hairy, dirty, stinky, and with eyes glowing bright red in the half-light of night, the monster was snuffling about the counter, knocking over everything in its path. Not finding what it wanted, it began to mutter a terrifying oath: 'I smells me a dog. I know he's here. When I finds 'im, I'll scrunch 'im, I'll munch 'im and I'll eat 'im all up!'"

"I couldn't believe my eyes and ears! 'This thing wants to eat me,' I silently screamed, 'so it must be a Wompus!' And with that, my heart raced wildly, my pulse pounded like a hammer on an anvil, every hair on my body stood on end and I thought I would barf. I wanted to sound the alarm, but no barks would come. I wanted to spring to the attack, but no muscles would move. I was frozen by fear, unable to perform my duty."

"Luckily for me, Master John turned on the light and the Wompus fled through the kitchen window. As he shut the window behind the

7

fiend, Master John poked fun at my weakness in the face of the enemy. His words were in jest, but I knew the painful truth – I was no better than a yellow-bellied coward!"

"Word of my disgrace spread quickly. Every dog on Moore Hill went out of its way to mock me. Contempt and ridicule became my painful lot in life, and I sank so low that I lost my pride."

"Forlorn and in need of some company, I took to hanging out with the bad dogs of the valley, down at the Dirty Dawg Saloon. Yes, little pups, it's true what the elders tell you about the Dirty Dawg – that place is the devil's den, alright. But it was there that I met the one true love of my life. Her name was Hot Chocolate and the moment I laid eyes on her I could see why! Hot Chocolate was the prettiest Lab imaginable, for she was sleek and graceful as she strolled amongst the customers, charming all she passed. I dreamt of that brown beauty day and night and wondered if she would ever love me as I loved her."

"But, alas, my love for Hot Chocolate was only one-sided. The awful truth struck like a bolt of lightening the night she sashayed up and whispered in my ear, 'Ooo, la, la, big boy! All the fellas love Hot Chocolate. Don't you?' In an instant, my jaw dropped, my tongue fell out the side of my mouth and I began to drool. The next thing I knew I was on my back, feet in the air and looking like a dying cockroach. Doggone, did I feel foolish, lying there in a posture of submission and Hot Chocolate laughing away!"

"To make matters worse, a bird dog jumped onto the bar and barked loudly for attention. He pointed a paw straight at me and said, 'That's him, that's Franklin, the coward of Moore Hill!' Howls of derision rang out as I slunk to the door to escape the relentless ridicule."

"But the worst was still to come. For when I finally reached the exit, I heard the most beautiful dog in the world sarcastically say, 'Franklin's just a silly pup, fellas. He's to be pitied, not scorned.'

And that's when I knew that Hot Chocolate didn't love me, for the dog of my dreams now made fun of me, too. I was crestfallen!"

"A feeling of great despair came over me and I never wanted to be near another dog as long as I lived! Oh, Mistress Carol and Master John still loved me, but the dogs of the hill and the flatland made me feel ashamed and inadequate. Unfortunately, my thoughts of worthlessness grew stronger still, for Master John wanted me to be a sled dog. But having lost all self-confidence, I couldn't do it; I was too insecure to even try. So, Master John started bringing home those dogs in the pen over yonder. He said he only needed them to pull his sled, but I knew better. I was convinced he'd lost all respect for me. Life became hopeless! All was lost!"

The audience of young dogs was so moved by Franklin's trials that not a dry eye could be seen among them. Nevertheless, they pulled themselves together, for they were compelled to hear what happened next.

"When I was feeling as low as a cat with no legs, I recollected the troubled days of my youth. How did I get through hard times before? How did I overcome misfortune back then? After much agonizing thought, I found the answer when ol' Jack's words flooded my mind. 'Every dog has his day. Every dog has his day.' Those words of hope had saved me once before; could they do it again? I'd already had one day; could I have another?"

"Then, one recent night, my questions were answered in an unexpected way. As I lay half asleep by an open window, I caught a whiff of the most revolting odor a dog will ever know — the unmistakable reek of Wompuses. Yes, I said Wompuses, young pups, for there were two of them stinkers and they were plotting to attack the sled dogs. 'We smells us some dogs,' chanted the Wompuses, 'we know they're here. When we finds 'em, we'll scrunch 'em, we'll munch 'em and we'll eat 'em all up!'"

"Without giving it a thought, I moved so quickly that the Wompuses didn't see me coming. Fast as a bullet, I hurled myself at the nearest devil, caught him below the shoulder and bowled him over. Like a hound possessed, I lunged at the second demon, but he knocked me crazier than a coyote. Feeling punch-drunk and helpless, I knew I was a sure goner as the Wompuses moved in to finish me off."

"But it was then that an amazing thing happened: the sled dogs started to howl like a pack of blood-thirsty wolves! 'Ow-ooool, ow-ooool, ow-ooool!' they cried. 'Ow-ooool, ow-ooool, ow-ooool!' Since the wolf is a predator every animal instinctively fears, the Wompuses were momentarily stunned, while I was startled to my senses. Again, I sprang to the attack, but I met head-to-head with a Wompus and knocked myself silly."

"Groggy and weak from the head butt, I lay motionless as the Wompuses came in for the kill. But just as those foul critters were about to pounce, the sled dogs howled again, and it was more chilling and terrifying than before. 'Ow-ooool, ow-ooool, ow-ooool!' they chanted. 'Ow-ooool, ow-ooool, ow-ooool!'"

"Fortunately for me, that last chorus of eerie howls did the trick. The bloodcurdling racket scared the fight out of the Wompuses, so they tucked their tails and ran. And as they fled into the night, I heard the smelly things swear that they'd never return to Moore Hill!"

As soon as Franklin ended his astonishing tale, the puppies began to celebrate his victory. They started by facing skyward and barking their version of a howling wolf: "oool, oool, oool," they sang, "oool, oool, oool!" Then they scampered to the sled dog pen and politely bowed to each dog inside – a show of respect for those near kin of the fearsome wolf. After that, the pups honored Franklin by promising to bark the memory of his brave deed, far and wide. Then they finished their tribute to him with a pledge – a pledge to become heroes someday, just like Franklin.

As the puppy pandemonium subsided, Franklin called the youngsters together, for he wanted them to hear the lesson his difficult life had taught him.

"When I was a young dog, I, too, dreamed of performing a heroic act and wished for my moment of glory. However, life has shown me that a great deed is not the only road to heroism. In fact, little ones, each of us can be a hero every day. For heroism also comes from having the courage to hope, the bravery to follow a dream, the strength to overcome our fears, the boldness to make our own path in life and the power to know right from wrong."

The puppies enthusiastically nodded agreement with Franklin's wise counsel, and then barked their desire to hear more from the big, brown dog. Not wanting to disappoint them, Franklin finished with the key to his hard-earned success.

"Now that you know how to become a hero, I have one last suggestion for you whelps. When times get tough and you're in need of some comfort, just call on the words of ol' Jack. 'Every dog has his day,' said Jack. "Every dog has his day.' If you repeat those words often and believe in their magic, then I guarantee you'll become a dog like me – a dog who's been lucky enough to have more than one."

Some tales are make-believe and some tales have actually happened. You can rest assured, dear reader, that everything in this tale is true — whether it happened or not.

Rules for
BIG DOGS

Story by **Clint Heverly**

Painting by **Denise Eileen Thurman**

Some tales are make-believe and some tales have actually happened. You can rest assured, dear reader, that everything in this tale is true — whether it happened or not.

It's a well known fact that one's quest for adulthood will be full of challenges. It's equally well known that one's character will be shaped by those trying times. And so it was for a tiny Pekinese puppy, named Fritz, as he pursued his dream — a dream to become a Big Dog.

"Achoo, achoo, aaa-choooo!" sneezed Fritz the Pekinese puppy as he lay in his bed, covers pulled up to his chin for safety.

"That was the scariest bedtime story you ever told me, Ivan. I'll never get to sleep after hearing about the Lost Dogs of Second Mountain!" complained a terrified Fritz.

After two more very wet and very loud sneezes, Fritz spoke again.

"One of those Lost Dogs could be under my bed right now, just waiting to kidnap me and roast me for dinner! Please look under the bed, Ivan, and make sure none of those crazy critters are hiding there! Please, please, please?"

A few violent sneezes later, Fritz's older brother, Ivan, gently laid a paw along Fritz's head and, in a reassuring voice, tried to calm his pint-sized brother.

"Don't be frightened little buddy, I'll protect you. That's what big brothers are supposed to do. That's what family is all about.

Besides, there's no truth in the tale of pup-nappin' Lost Dogs from Second Mountain. It's just a make-believe bedtime story told to frighten youngsters like you. Anyway, Fritz, do you remember what I taught you? What should you do if you get scared?"

"Well, you're supposed to bark, bark loudly and wildly!" exclaimed Fritz.

"That's right, little brother," applauded Ivan, "when you get scared, bark loudly and wildly. Your bark is not only an alarm and a cry for help, it's a weapon of self-defense, too. Now, suppose I was a Lost Dog who wanted to take you prisoner. What should you do?"

"Yip, yip, yip." barked Fritz rather weakly. "Yip, yip, yip."

"That bark's not bad, little bro," offered Ivan, trying to be positive, "but I think you can do better. Try this; ruff, ruff, ruff!" barked Ivan ferociously. "Ruff, ruff, ruff!"

Wanting to be like his big brother, because he admired him so, Fritz gamely tried again – a bit louder this time. "Arf, arf, arf! Arf, arf, arf!"

"You're getting better, Fritz, better with every bark!" praised Ivan. "We'll keep working on it. Now, let's go to sleep and rest up for tomorrow's Sniffabout."

But Fritz wasn't ready to sleep, for he had an important question to ask his big brother, a question he posed in a most serious tone of voice.

"Before we say goodnight, Ivan, would you please explain 'the gift?'"

"Certainly, little buddy," answered Ivan. "As I told you last night, everyone has a special talent we Big Dogs call 'the gift.' A step on the path to growing up requires a pup like you to attend a Sniffabout and discover his gift. And once he learns what his gift is, he must use it to benefit others."

"I think I understand now, big brother," said Fritz. "Find what you're really good at doing and use it to help others. Do you think I'll find my gift tomorrow?" asked a worried Fritz.

"Absolutely, little fella," assured Ivan. "That's why I invited you to the Sniffabout."

And with those soothing words from Ivan – along with one last check under the bed for Lost Dogs – Fritz's fears disappeared, his sneezes ceased and he passed into a sound sleep where he dreamt of becoming a Big Dog.

Fritz and Ivan were brothers by another mother, for they were not litter mates, not even the same breed of dog. Ivan, an 85 lb. hound, was a tall, lean and stately dog of unknown ancestry. Some thought him Swiss Mountain Dog, while others said he had a lot of Beagle in him. Whatever his pedigree, Ivan looked downright sleek and handsome. He possessed a short and shiny brown, black and white coat, white socks and a white tipped tail. Although sometimes shy and aloof, and usually a dog of few words, Ivan exuded strength and confidence as he patrolled his mountaintop domain.

Fritz, a tiny Pekinese puppy – a dog bred by the ancient Chinese to look like a miniature lion – was just the opposite of Ivan. In stature, Fritz was truly the little brother. Only about a foot and half long and about 11 inches high as he stood on all fours, he may have weighed 10 lbs. soaking wet. Mostly white in color, with some blonde, gray and black woven in, Fritz wore a long, flowing mane of a coat which waved wonderfully in the wind when he ran. He was full of energy and, like any young dog, he could be a pest of a pup – extremely talkative, rambunctious and often downright obnoxious. Oh, and as strange as it may seem, he had an odd trait that only surfaced when he got scared. Being frightened made Fritz sneeze – very loud, very frequent, very wet sneezes – just like the sneezes he had when Ivan told him the bedtime tale of the Lost Dogs.

The next day dawned bright and cool on First Mountain, the place where Ivan and Fritz lived with their mistress, Bernadette. The area was heavily forested and provided endless places for a curious dog to investigate. Even better, it was sparsely populated, making it the perfect playground where dogs could roam free without their owners in tow. Although Ivan was usually up at the crack of dawn, on this day, an excited Fritz awoke first.

Fritz was especially energized this morning because today was Sniffabout day; a day he would accompany Ivan and his hilltop buddies on his first journey of adventure. More importantly for Fritz, the Sniffabout would also be a test, a test to learn if he was ready to move from puppyhood to Big Dog status. If Fritz passed the Sniffabout, he would gain pack membership, and hence a second family, a dog family – a prize every pup coveted. One way or another, it would be a day filled with learning for the young Peke. Fritz found Ivan asleep on the stairs and nudged him awake. Then they scampered to the bedroom and awoke Mistress Bernadette, got her to open the kitchen door and off they flew to meet the First Mountain pack.

Fritz and Ivan were the first to reach the top of the ridge and the trail that led along it. As they waited for the pack's arrival, Ivan reviewed the time-tested Rules for Big Dogs with Fritz.

"Don't forget, little brother, if you want to earn pack membership, then you must act like a Big Dog. Let's go over the rules so you remember how to behave. OK, Fritz, can you FAART like a Big Dog?"

"Yes, yes, I can FAART!" replied an exuberant Fritz. "Just listen to this one! *'F, F = FAMILY: honoring and protecting one's family are the greatest good. A, A = ALARM: don't hesitate to bark an alarm; act cautiously when you hear one. A, A = ATTITUDE: always keep trying; never give up. R, R = RESPECT: respect for others should be freely given; respect from others must be earned. T, T = THINK: think through a problem before you act.'"*

After his perfect recitation of the Rules for Big Dogs, Fritz proudly asked, "So, how did I do, big brother? How's my FAARTing?"

"Bravo, Fritz, you've learned the rules well!" praised Ivan. "Now, if you can remember to FAART when necessary, then you should do just fine on the Sniffabout. Oh, I almost forgot, Fritz. Here's a rule of my own, one that I've found very useful over the years. Add the letter O. '*O = OBEY: obey your elders, but obey your inner dog before all others.*' Your inner dog is that little voice inside that guides you in difficult situations, and you must learn to trust it."

"I think I've got it, big bro!" shouted Fritz. "I'll just FAART and add an O. FAART-O, FAART-O, FAART-O", chanted little Fritz, "FAART-O, FAART-O, FAART-O."

As they finished their review of the Rules for Big Dogs, the rest of the pack showed up, tails wagging and tongues panting in anticipation of Sniffabout day. And what a fine collection of hounds they were. There was Hunter, a stubby tailed Beagle; he had a super sense of smell and the prettiest of yelps when tracking a scent. There was Marley, a midsized Black Lab who was in search of a new family and had recently fallen in with the pack on a trial basis; she had a quick temper, but she possessed the valuable talent of sensing and pointing out trouble before it happened. Then there was Josh, a huge Golden Retriever who was as gentle as they come; he was a legend among the pack because he had eaten a pound of nails when he was 6 months old and had lived to tell about it! Kingston, the eldest and wisest of the group, was a large Black Lab/Collie mix with a white mark on his chest; he was revered by his mates because he was never rude – always the gentleman. Lastly, there was Tuffy; she was part Terrier, part Chihuahua and a true athlete who could climb anything – even a tree! Being a Pekinese pup, Fritz was the smallest, as well as, the youngest dog present. Ivan was neither the tallest, nor the largest, but he possessed the gift of leadership, and hence was accepted as "alpha dog" — the leader of the pack. Unfortunately for Ivan, it did not take long for his gift of management to be tested this day.

"Nobody told me the midget Peke was coming along!" grumbled Marley. "I guarantee he'll be nothing but trouble!"

Hearing Marley's complaint, Fritz lost his manners and snapped back at her.

"My big brother, Ivan, invited me, and if you don't like it, Marley, why don't you challenge his leadership? Bet you're too scared! Bet you're nothing but a fraidycat!"

Extremely offended by being compared to a cat — and a scared cat, at that — Marley moved to give Fritz a swat for his impertinence. However, Ivan intervened in the spat, sided with Marley and chastised little Fritz.

"Fritz, 'to belittle is to be little.' You tried to embarrass Marley with your taunts, but you've made yourself look small, instead. If you want to become a Big Dog, then you must respect others. Now, apologize to Marley for your rude remarks."

On hearing Ivan's reprimand, Fritz recalled the "R" rule; respect for others must be freely given; respect from others must be earned. Realizing that he had made a huge mistake, Fritz hung his head in shame for quite sometime. But, eventually, he looked up at Ivan and mumbled the words, "I'm sorry."

"Louder!" demanded Ivan. "And say it like you mean it!"

Fritz hung his head again — longer this time. Then he slowly looked up at Marley and spoke loudly enough for all to hear: "Marley, I'm very sorry for my disrespectful words. It won't happen again."

Marley growled in anger at Fritz, and then glared at Ivan as if demanding more punishment for the impertinent Peke. But wise Ivan ignored Marley and said, "Mates, it takes a Big Dog to admit his mistakes and apologize for them. Fritz has spunk, and he is ready and willing to learn. Let him come with us. What do you say?"

The group talked it over and agreed that Ivan was an excellent alpha dog, and that should count for something. So, by each holding up a paw – even Marley, of all dogs – the pack signified its approval of Ivan's request.

"Good!" declared Ivan. "Now, it's time to start the Sniffabout, test the little guy and have some fun!"

To soften Marley's anger, Ivan appointed her lead dog for the Sniffabout, while he and Fritz would bring up the rear. Then, with wagging tails held high, the pack set out to find adventure and to learn if Fritz was ready for Big Dog status. However, as his tiff with Marley had already shown, Fritz's search for adulthood would not be an easy one. In fact, the little Peke's quest was about to get much, much harder.

No more than a few hundred yards down the trail, Fritz encountered his second test of the day. It began when Marley used her gift of pointing. She froze in a posture where she leaned slightly forward, with her tail and nose straight out and her right forepaw lifted and bent at the knee – her entire body pointing toward invisible trouble. Hunter saw her point, immediately smelled the problem and barked up a warning: "Porcupine up ahead. Gang way!" The cry went up from dog to dog: "Porcupine up ahead. Gang way!" To avoid prickly trouble, each dog veered off the trail and out of harm's way. Well, each dog except Fritz, that is, for Fritz just had to see what all the fuss was about.

Instead of obeying Hunter's alarm, Fritz stayed on the trail and ran smack-dab into a porcupine! Having scented the dogs in advance, the porc had raised its quills in readiness for battle. "Wap. Wap. Wap," was the sound of the porc's quills as they struck Fritz in the right front leg.

"Arf, arf, arf!" screamed Fritz. "I've been hit with stickers! Arf, arf, arf!"

In the worst pain of his life, an injured Fritz limped back to the pack as quickly as he could. Luckily for him, Kingston possessed the gift of healing and knew exactly what to do. Some of the quills had barely broken the skin, so Kingston easily pulled them out. However, others had entered so deeply that they had to be pushed all the way through the little dog's leg!

"Ouch! Ouch! Ouch!" screamed Fritz. "Ouch! Ouch! Ouch!"

As Kingston showed Fritz how to lick his wounds to soothe the soreness, Marley expressed her discontent with the Peke's misbehavior, once again.

"What did I tell you?" griped Marley. "He's nothing but trouble. First, he disrespected me, and now he has disobeyed an alarm. He should be sent home – pronto!"

"No, no, no!" pleaded Fritz. "You'll see. I'll listen better next time. Honest, honest I will!"

Josh and Tuffy wagged their heads in disbelief of Fritz' plea, but wise Kingston spoke in his defense.

"Mates, we all made mistakes in our younger days, but that's how we learned right from wrong. Experience is always the best teacher. So, I say the pup deserves another chance."

After a brief discussion, the pack agreed that Kingston was the wisest dog present, and that should count for something. So, without another word spoken, Marley trotted off and the other dogs followed in single file, yipping and sniffing as they travelled along the trail. Poor little Fritz brought up the rear – limping and whimpering from the quill wounds to his leg.

After quite some time had passed, the pack grew weary. So, it stopped to rest, and Fritz's next test soon followed. In her desire to get even for Fritz's belittling taunts, Marley challenged him to eat from a mound of brown balls piled nearby.

"Go ahead, Fritz, eat them," coaxed Marley. "I know you're hungry. They taste just like the kibble your mom feeds you."

Always famished, Fritz moved to eat some pellets. But just as he was about to take a bite, Josh barked a warning: "Don't eat that stuff, Fritz, it's deer poop!"

Marley scowled at Josh for ruining her trick. Then she headed off, again, and each dog followed. Well, each dog except Fritz, that is, for Fritz just had to taste the deer droppings since they looked a lot like kibble!

"Ooh! Ooh! Ooh! That tastes foul!" exclaimed Fritz. "Ooh! Ooh! Ooh!"

Ivan heard Fritz's complaint, circled back and then scolded him for breaking two rules this time – disobeying a warning from Josh and acting without thinking of the consequences. So, once again, Fritz hung his head in shame, apologized for his actions and begged for forgiveness.

After much debate, the pack decided that Fritz could continue the Sniffabout, for he still had a good attitude, and that should count for something. Thankful for another chance, little Fritz limped and spit his way down the path, wondering all the while if he would ever find his gift and FAART like a Big Dog.

The next test for Fritz came soon thereafter. Marley abruptly halted, went into pointing mode and barked out a warning: "Swamp ahead! Watch for quicksand! Step lively!" The word passed down from dog to dog: "Swamp ahead! Watch for quicksand! Step lively!" As the dogs approached the mire, they managed to skirt around it. Well, all the dogs except Fritz, that is!

When Fritz saw the water, all he could think about was washing the taste of deer poop from his mouth. Alarm, or no alarm, he had to have a drink. So, he carelessly waded into the swamp and began lapping water. But, unfortunately, he also got stuck in the quicksand below. He struggled to escape from the sticky muck, but the suction worked against him – the harder he tried to free himself, the faster he sank. In big trouble again, Fritz barked for help. "Arf, arf, arf!" Then louder. "Arf, arf, arf!"

The pack heard Fritz's distress call, circled back to the swamp and found the little Peke up to his neck in icky, sticky, gooey mud! This time, Josh, the Golden Retriever, used his gift of fetching to help the wayward pup. Josh placed a long stick in his mouth, lay on his stomach and inched cautiously forward. When he could get no closer, he extended the rod and told Fritz to bite hard and hold fast. The little pup clamped down on the stick and big Josh pulled him to dry land, where Fritz lay panting, exhausted from his near-death experience.

Ivan, of course, was elated that his little brother was safe. But he was also extremely angry. Fritz had disobeyed the rules, again, and had nearly lost his life for doing so.

"That's it little brother, that does it! You've broken every FAARTing rule on the list! It's time to take you home while you're still alive!"

Fritz leapt to his feet to plead his case, but before he could utter a word, Marley – of all dogs – spoke for him.

"Fritz is a gamer, Ivan. There's no quit in him. I say we all keep going."

Fritz looked to Ivan and then to the pack for permission to continue. After much consultation, the dogs reluctantly consented, for Marley had stuck up for Fritz, and that should count for something. So, off they trotted, again, with Marley in the lead and Fritz bringing up the rear – exhausted, limping, spitting, occasionally shaking mud from his coat and chanting "FAART-O, FAART-O, FAART-O" as if it were a magic spell. Unbeknownst to the pack, Fritz would need some powerful magic in the test that lay ahead.

The pack meandered down the trail until it encountered a high wall of stone in its path; a problem that caused the dogs to halt and mull it over. Should they try to climb the cliff, or should they turn and head for home? Each dog had his say and all agreed to climb. Not much larger than Fritz, but as sure footed as a burro, Tuffy volunteered her gift to the cause.

"Let me go first, amigos, and I'll find us a way to the top," offered Tuffy.

The pack gave quick approval to Tuffy's request, for she could scale a tree, and that should count for something. So, up, up, up she went, cautiously picking and choosing her footing as she climbed the steep face. After a few minutes, and a misstep or two, Tuffy was successful and stood on the rim above.

"Okay, mates, I showed you the easiest way up!" shouted Tuffy. "Careful, though, some of the rocks are loose!"

One at a time, they duplicated Tuffy's trail; first Josh, then Hunter, followed by Kingston, Ivan and then Marley. But when Marley took her turn, she intentionally loosened some stones as she made her climb. Now, it was little Fritz's turn, and one false step could cost him his life.

Tired, dirty, thirsty and sore, Fritz started his climb. Up, up, up he went – slowly at first, then more rapidly as he gained confidence. And just as Fritz was about to reach the top, he stepped on a loose stone, lost his footing and started to fall!

Down, down, down he went, flipping head over heels toward certain disaster! But just as he was about to hit the ground, Fritz somehow gained control of his body. He landed on all fours and his little legs absorbed the shock of the long fall.

Stunned by his hard landing, Fritz was frozen in place for quite some time. Eventually, though, he came to his senses, shook himself off and assessed his limbs. And as you might imagine, he was thrilled to find that all of his parts were in good working order!

The pack was also delighted that Fritz wasn't hurt, and called for him to climb again. Shaken, but still determined, Fritz took several deep breaths to calm his fears. Then he summoned his courage and tried anew. Up, up, up he went, reaching the top without mishap this time. And now that his dangerous climb was over, the dogs had a new-found respect for the Pekinese pup.

"See, I was right!" gushed Marley. "Fritz is a gamer! There's no quit in him, nosiree! I say his never-give-up attitude deserves a reward. Let's put him at #2 in line – just behind me."

The pack gave instant approval to Marley's request, for it finally realized the little Peke would never give up, and that should count for something. So, once again, they set out, with Fritz at #2 for the first time today – just behind Marley. But unbeknownst to the pack, that's exactly what Marley needed. For she knew that great danger lurked ahead, and she planned to get Fritz into a jam he wouldn't get out of this time.

A few minutes further on, Marley got her chance to even the score with the pesky Pekinese puppy. At just the right spot on the trail, she veered from the beaten path – sight unseen – and Fritz unconsciously followed her into a large thicket. And once the other dogs had passed on by, Marley herded little Fritz to a nearby cave and right into big trouble!

"Fritz, to prove that you're a Big Dog, I want you to search inside this cave for food and water. Report back A.S.A.P.," ordered Marley.

Marley's command created a big dilemma for little Fritz. His inner dog said "no," but his desire to obey an elder said "go." After some thought – and a nudge from Marley – he half-heartedly entered the cave. It was damp and slimy inside and there was a disgusting odor, too, so his inner dog caused Fritz to turn back. But just a few steps into his retreat, he was nabbed by a giant paw and raised high into the air. As his eyes adjusted to the dim light of the cave, little Fritz found himself face-to-face with the largest, the hairiest and the scariest critter he had ever seen!

Meanwhile, certain that Fritz had met his end, Marley ran off to alert the pack. And just as she reached the trail, the other dogs showed up and, of course, immediately inquired about Fritz.

"I'm sorry, Ivan, but your brother disobeyed me and went off on his own," lied Marley. "I searched for him, but lost his track."

"What's the general direction?" asked Hunter. As Marley pointed toward the cave, Hunter put his gift to work and, in no time at all, barked out, "I've got his scent, mates, follow me!" Then, quick as a bullet, he made a beeline to the cave, with the pack hot on his heels.

When Ivan spotted the cave, he did not hesitate to act. "Protecting one's family is the greatest good," he told himself. So, in total disregard of his own safety, Ivan rushed into the dark hole and ran smack-dab into a 500 lb. bear!

Brave Ivan charged the huge creature, but the bear easily swatted him to the cave floor and pinned him there. Ivan twisted and turned, howled and growled, barked and snarled, but he could not loose himself from the massive beast. Growing weak from his struggle, and fearing the end was near for Fritz and himself, he barked a last goodbye to his brother.

"I love ya, little Fritz! Always remember your Rules for Big Dogs – just FAART and add an O. See you on the other side!"

And with that, the hungry bear began to salivate, for she planned to begin dinner with Fritz as an appetizer, followed by Ivan as the main course! But seeing the bear lick its lips terrified Fritz, and caused him to do what he always did when he got really scared — Fritz started to sneeze.

"Achoo, achoo, aaah-chooo!" sneezed Fritz — loud, powerful, slobber-filled sneezes. "Achoo, achoo, aaah-chooo!" he sneezed — right into the face of his hungry captor. And, as luck would have it, his disgusting sneezes befuddled the bear, and gave Fritz one last chance to save himself.

"FAART-O, FAART-O, FAART-O," chanted Fritz as he searched for a quick solution to his life-or-death situation. *"FAMILY, ALARM, ATTITUDE, RESPECT, OBEY.* What should I do? What can I do?"

As the Rules for Big Dogs crossed his mind, Fritz's inner dog hit on an idea. It was an idea so clever that it triggered an extraordinary FAART! It was a FAART so surprising that it caused two miracles!

The first miracle happened when Fritz found his gift and started to roar like lion. Yes, that's right! The little Pekinese pup that was bred to look like a lion began to roar like one! And his roars were the loudest and wildest you've ever heard!

"RROOAARR! RROOAARR! RROOAARR!" bellowed Fritz. "RROOAARR! RROOAARR! RROOAARR!"

The second miracle occurred when the bear became confused, for how could roars so huge come from a dog so small? It lifted its leg from Ivan and dropped Fritz to the ground, and the two lucky dogs made their escape! Out the den door they ran, quick as lightening, the pack racing behind them. Down the trail they flew, like the wind, to the steep wall they had climbed. Down the steep slope they slid, one at a time, as rapidly as they dared. Then down the trail they scrambled, skirted the quicksand, dodged the porcupine and tumbled off the ridge as they reached the safety of home.

"Well, well, well, mates, did Fritz prove to be a Big Dog today, or what!" boasted a proud Ivan as the dogs regrouped. "He got off to a slow start, but he completed the Sniffabout, outsmarted a bear and saved my life. What more could a pup do to deserve pack membership?"

"I'll tell you what he could do!" groused Marley, still angry that Fritz had been tested for pack membership before she was. "He could learn to follow the rules, that's what he could do!"

With that, Fritz limped over to Marley and called her out.

"You're a dirty dog, Marley! You wanted to get even with me 'cause I called you a fraidycat. So, you led me to the bear cave, ordered me to go inside and hoped I'd be eaten by that monster!"

On hearing Fritz's accusation, Ivan stood toe-to-toe with Marley and asked, "Is that true, Marley? Did you intentionally lead Fritz astray and into harm's way?"

"What difference does it make?" snorted Marley. "He's too puny, too stupid and too obnoxious to help the pack anyway!"

And with that, Marley pounced like a crazed cat and sunk her canines into the little guy's neck. But just as quickly, the other dogs jumped into the fray and wrestled her away from Fritz. As the pack pinned Marley to the ground, Ivan charged her with a serious offense.

"Marley, seeking revenge against Fritz has made you blind, for you cannot see that an attack against him is also an attack on the pack. The pack is your family, Marley, and it's more important than any one dog. Your behavior has been selfish and dangerous and, for that, you should be expelled. What do you say, mates? Does she go, or does she stay?"

Without hesitation, the pack turned one paw down against Marley, and then stepped back, allowing her to rise. With a tear in her eye because she had lost another family, Marley slunk back up First Mountain – not to be heard of again for a long, long while.

When Marley had passed out of sight, Ivan began the ritual to make Fritz a pack member. He assembled his troops in true pack fashion – oldest to youngest – and then closely inspected each one. Finding every dog to be satisfactory, he requested that Kingston present the award. Then Ivan commanded, "Front and center, little Fritz!"

The youngster proudly pranced forward – tongue panting, tail wagging and head held high in anticipation of his prize. With Fritz at center stage, Kingston began his speech with some thoughts about Marley.

"As you well know, mates, we call a dog without a pack a Lost Dog – a dog who will not have the love and support a good family provides. Marley did not obey the Rules for Big Dogs, and is now a Lost Dog because of it. What a shame, what a pity, because somewhere inside of Marley is a dog who knows better."

Then Kingston walked over to Fritz, gently laid a huge paw on the tiny Peke's shoulder and finished his address.

"Marley's misbehavior and your own childish actions caused you much grief today, Fritz. Nevertheless, you kept a good attitude, refused to give up and, most importantly, you found your gift. Your gift not only saved you from certain death, young pup, but it saved a family member, too – the highest good a dog can do."

"Fritz, you have proven today that you can FAART like a Big Dog. Because of that, you have earned our respect, passed your Sniffabout and gained pack membership, too. You may be small in size, little Fritz, but like the mighty lion, you are large in heart. You are truly a Big Dog now!"

Some tales are make-believe and some tales have actually happened. You can rest assured, dear reader, that everything in this tale is true — whether it happened or not.

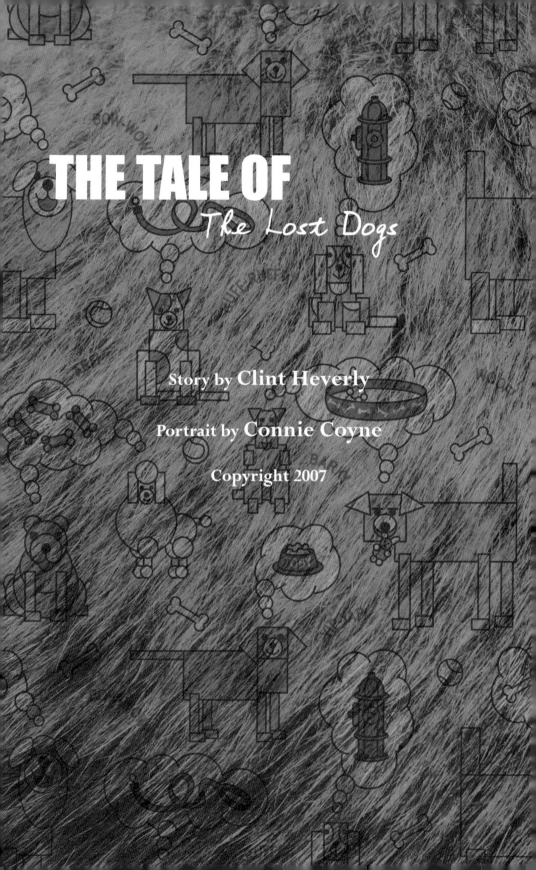

THE TALE OF
The Lost Dogs

Story by **Clint Heverly**

Portrait by **Connie Coyne**

Copyright 2007

Some tales are make-believe and some tales have actually happened. You can rest assured, dear reader, that everything in this tale is true — whether it happened or not.

"There is a great paradox regarding true love — all of us crave it, yet few of us know how to get it and fewer still know when it's gotten." **(Marley)**

Not so long ago, a classic black Labrador retriever, named Marley, paced and sniffed the perimeter of her property looking for lizards. She poked under the patio furniture — nothing there. She searched the flower pots lining the deck — no luck. She marched into the yard and inspected the metal fish planter — no success either. She checked the nearby birdhouse for the orange-headed lizard living there — nothing doing. If you watched Marley on lizard patrol you'd think that she was just a simple-minded creature with nothing of consequence in her head besides chasing lizards. However, if you thought that about Marley, you'd be wrong — dead wrong — for Marley was quite capable of deep thought, and her mind was full of haunting memories and frightening experiences.

Tiring of lizard patrol, Marley moved to the inside of her new house, a gorgeous home owned by her latest family, Susan and Albert. She lay on her bed in front of the fireplace and gazed at a portrait of her and Albert walking the beach of Hilton Head Island — an artwork Susan had commissioned just for them. The likeness was amazingly accurate, and Marley heard tell it was featured in a magazine ad: *"It* doesn't get much better than walking down the beach with one of your very best friends," read the ad. *"Turn that special moment into a portrait destined to become a family heirloom."*

Truth be known, the first thing Marley did each day was stare at the painting and thank her lucky stars for the good life she now enjoyed. For, you see, Marley had been part of several families before Susan and Albert rescued her from the animal shelter, and all of those relationships ended badly for her.

After a brief siesta by the fireplace, she ambled outside to the deck, again. As she lay there watching some golfers just beyond her yard, Marley drifted into an extremely deep sleep, and dreamt of the time that her family was a pack of hounds from Hell, the Lost Dogs of Second Mountain — the worst family a dog could ever have!

To follow this tale, you must understand two important truths. First, you must recognize that a Lost Dog is a dog without a good family. Secondly, you must grasp that a pup usually becomes a Lost Dog through no fault of its own. This is how it happens.

It's a fact that a puppy dog's experiences in its first few months are the most formative in its upbringing. During this time, a pup must bond with other animals, pick up social skills and learn to be house broken, too. A young dog needs consistent and logical training to acquire good habits. Otherwise, it may become confused, unhappy, overly aggressive, or too submissive.

It's also fact that many humans are poor trainers. They do not reward good behavior and they punish bad behavior too long after it happens. A dog trapped in a bad learning environment never gets properly trained. Instead, it becomes lost — lost to itself and lost to its owner. Unsocialized, untrained, and unloved, the dog often becomes unwanted through no fault of its own. In short, it turns into a Lost Dog, and a Lost Dog is a sad thing, a sad thing indeed.

Now that you know what a Lost Dog is, you must also know that Marley could've been a poster-pup for the Lost Dogs of this world.

Lacking proper care, training and affection from her original owners, and overhearing them talk of "putting her down," Marley ran away from home the first chance she got. She ran and she ran and she did not slow down until she reached First Mountain. It was there, as luck would have it, that she ran right into her next family – the First Mountain pack.

The First Mountain pack was led by Ivan, a fearless Swiss Mountain dog. Ivan's mates included Tuffy, a Terrier/Chihuahua mix; Josh, a huge Golden Retriever; Hunter, a stubby tailed Beagle; and Kingston, a combination of Collie and Black Lab. Sensing the First Mountain dogs before she actually saw them, Marley involuntarily went into danger alert mode. She froze in a posture where she leaned slightly forward, with nose and tail straight out and right forepaw lifted and bent at the knee – her entire body pointing toward trouble.

The First Mountain dogs had never seen a pointing pup before, so they investigated Marley by performing up-close-and-personal sniffs – as dogs are fond of doing. It could have been a volatile situation, but wise Ivan defused it by asking, in a humorous tone of voice, "What in the world is this black Lab doing, and why is she doing it?" With that, the pack began to giggle and so did Marley. Feeling at ease from the sound of laughter, Marley introduced herself, and then offered an explanation for the odd pose.

"I call it pointing. It's something I've instinctively done since puppyhood. When I feel danger on the wind, I stop and point it out. In this case, you guys were the potential threat. Weird, huh?"

However, Kingston, the eldest and the wisest of the pack, thought better.

"Well, yeah, it's strange, alright. But your unique skill could be quite useful to a pack of dogs. Do you already have a pack?"

"I don't have a family right now, and I sort of like it that way," replied Marley, trying her best to appear self-reliant. "But I guess I could give your pack a try, if you really want me to."

With that, Ivan presented the following motion: "I move that Marley be accepted into the pack on probationary status. All in favor raise a paw."

The pack raised a collective paw to show its approval, and Marley was secretly overjoyed – she had found another family!

Marley and her new mates met frequently to explore First Mountain. Life was good during those times, even for a homeless dog like her. But good times don't last forever, especially for a Lost Dog like Marley. It all started on the day Ivan brought his little brother along for a Sniffabout.

A Sniffabout, if you don't know, is both an adventure and a test for a prospective pack member. The pack brings in a new dog, allows it to accompany the group in search of adventure and examines the novice pup to see if it has the makings of a Big Dog – a dog ready for pack membership. On this particular Sniffabout, a little Pekinese puppy, named Fritz, would be tested for Big Dog qualities.

Stung by the possibility that Fritz might gain pack membership before she would, and hurt that she wasn't considered for membership before him, Marley flew into a jealous rage.

"Nobody told me the midget Peke was coming along," snarled Marley. "I guarantee he'll be nothing but trouble. Just look at his lack of size and that flat, ugly face. He's way too puny and too stupid looking to help the pack!"

Hearing this, little Fritz lost his manners and snapped back at Marley.

"My big brother, Ivan, invited me and if you don't like it, Marley, why don't you challenge his leadership? Bet you're afraid to try! Bet you're nothing but a scaredycat!"

Offended by being compared to a cat – and a scared cat, at that – Marley moved to give Fritz a swat for his impertinence. However, wise Ivan intervened in the quarrel, sided with Marley and made Fritz apologize.

"I'm really sorry for being disrespectful, Marley," lamented little Fritz. "It won't happen again."

Ivan sensed that Marley was still angry, so he appointed her Sniffabout leader in hopes of cheering her up. But Marley's terrible temper got in the way of the honor. Lead dog on the Sniffabout meant nothing at this point; all that really mattered now was getting even with Fritz. So, being a Lost Dog, and hence untrained to make good choices and proper decisions, Marley conceived a sinister plan, instead – a plan to gain revenge.

As Marley led the pack on the Sniffabout, she used every dirty trick she could think of to get even with Fritz. She started by guiding the pack into a porcupine and Fritz took several painful quills. On down the trail, she pointed out deer droppings to the tiny Peke and told him they were food. Fritz ate the deer poop and got the foulest taste imaginable in his mouth. Next, she directed the pack to a swamp where she just knew that Fritz would want a drink of water to clear his palate. The little fellow got stuck in the bog and almost drowned. After that, Marley took them to a steep wall of rock. When the pack decided to climb the cliff, Marley intentionally loosened some stones so Fritz might lose his footing and fall. Fritz took a nasty tumble, but somehow came through it unscathed. But Marley had one more ruse up her paw. She herded Fritz to an occupied bear den and ordered him to investigate inside. However, Fritz survived that terrible trick, too, and Marley was expelled from the pack for her evil conduct.

Banished from the pack – now friendless and without family for a second time – Marley became a Lost Dog, again. Tears filled her eyes and remorse filled her heart as she slunk away from the First Mountain troupe. "Why did I get so angry?" she asked herself. "Why did I have to be so mean? Isn't family and friendship more important than getting revenge?" But Marley could find no answers to her introspective questions, for she was a Lost Dog — a dog who doesn't know proper behavior.

Expelled from the First Mountain pack, Marley could do nothing but wander the peaks and valleys of Second Mountain in search of another family. She had been meandering for several weeks, despondent, hungry and weak, when she stumbled upon the oddest thing — several dishes of dog food and water sitting on the trail. Without giving it a thought, she dashed to the dishes, gobbled down some kibble and took a big gulp of water. But then it happened — she sensed danger and began to point!

And danger did not take long to appear! For the food was a trap and Marley was soon surrounded by the meanest, vilest and scruffiest dogs you've ever seen! Their mangy bodies were missing fur, their faces and backs were covered with horrible scars and sores, their coats were dirty and unkempt and they howled and snarled like a collection of cornered cats. Without explanation, those nasty critters pounced on Marley, bound her feet to a pole, tied a bandana over her eyes and carried her off.

As the band of crazed canines marched along, they tortured Marley — biting her ears and pulling her tail — all while chanting a most frightful song:

One day, or another, we're gonna gitcha, we'll gitcha, we'll gitcha, gitcha, gitcha!
One way, or another, we'll gitcha, we'll gitcha, we'll gitcha, gitcha, gitcha!

Enduring taunts, tortures and that eerie song, Marley was convinced the world had gone mad. But, unfortunately for Marley, greater insanity was still to come!

After a considerable hike to the camp of her captors, Marley was released from her blindfold and bindings. As she regained her senses, she was dragged into a well-lit cave and placed in front of the leader, a squat, 30 lb. French bulldog. Black in color, with a white patch on his chest, the bulldog wore a faded purple cape across his shoulders and a tri-cornered hat upon his head.

"Welcome to Second Mountain you sniveling whelp," barked the bulldog. "Now, bow before me and kiss my paw."

Seeing no choice, Marley complied, and the bulldog continued.

"The troops call me 'Your Highness,' but my real name's Bonaparte. What's your name, black Lab? What's your story?"

Learning Marley's name and history, Bonaparte then peppered her with questions about pointing. When finished, he held his hat over his heart and began a most passionate presentation.

"We call our army of troubled souls the Lost Dogs of Second Mountain, and we are on a most glorious mission – a mission to rid the world of cats. For if there are no cats, then humans will want us as their pets, instead!"

"A dog with a gift like yours, Marley, would greatly aid our fight. In return for your service, we offer you a new family – a family that will provide the love and security you search for."

Bonaparte halted his speech to adjust his cape – a task he completed with a flourish – and then continued his address.

"Battle is all we know, and the biggest battle is soon to come. Since one must take sides in war, Marley, one might as well choose the side that will be victorious, for it is always better to eat than be eaten!"

As Marley gulped at the thought of being some wild dog's dinner, Bonaparte donned his tri-cornered hat, dramatically pulled his cape across his chest and then finished his offer.

"I guarantee that the corpse of a cat will always smell sweet! So, what do you say, black Lab? Will you join our cause? You have 30 seconds to make a decision."

Seeing no choice, a frightened Marley gave a quick reply: "I do need a new family, Your Highness, so count me in."

"I knew you'd see things my way, Marley. Welcome to the Lost Dogs!" exclaimed a jubilant Bonaparte. "Now, an army marches on its stomach, so get some chow and put a little meat on your skinny bones. You may kiss my paw before you leave."

As she departed headquarters, Marley noticed that Bonaparte's camp was actually a fort of stone, for it was hemmed in by huge boulders. There was a main gate at one end, a smaller escape exit at the other, and sentinels stood guard atop the huge rocks that formed the perimeter. The entrance to Bonaparte's cave was located at the highest point of the camp and, from there, Marley was able to survey the entire base. And as she looked around, she started to shiver, for the bizarre place filled her with fear!

Populated by a gang of canine castoffs, the area looked more like a battlefield than a camp. The landscape was littered with empty food containers and dirty, torn blankets. Giant craters had been pawed into the dirt, and shards of gnawed bones and piles of dog poop covered the ground. Cages of cats were plentiful, and their woeful cries added an air of evil to the eerie scene. And Bonaparte's soldier-dogs — who seemed to be everywhere — acted more like lunatics in an asylum than an army on a mission!

There was a most aggressive dachshund that poked the air with a paw and foamed at the mouth as he ranted about cats. He was convinced that cats were the cause of the Lost Dogs' problems, and that the only solution — he called it the "Final Solution" — was feline extermination. "Today, Second Mountain!" he raved. "Tomorrow, a cat-less World!"

Marley then spotted a hairless Chinese crested who was surely the strangest looking dog in the universe. The crested was mostly furless, with a few tufts of silky-white hair on her head, ears, feet and the tip of her tail. Otherwise, her exterior was nothing but pink skin, dotted by spots of pigmentation. High spirited and domineering, the crested trotted about the camp, occasionally stopping to read from a small, red book of her sayings. "What difference does it make if the cat is black or white, so long as it is dead!" she quoted from her little red book. "Make those feline vermin understand that power grows from a gnashing of fangs!"

Marley's attention was then drawn to a gigantic Russian Bear schnauzer. Standing three feet tall and sporting a rough, black coat, the schnauzer seemed possessed by the devil as he gazed about with his hypnotizing eyes. He preached that cats were the "opium of the people" – selfish critters who controlled humans at the expense of dogs. "Lost Dogs of the world unite against cats!" he urged with fanatical fervor. "Lost Dogs of the world unite against cats!"

As if those three maniacs weren't menacing enough, Marley saw plenty more in this cast of crazed critters; dogs of every sort who delighted in performing the vilest acts – cooking and eating their captives being chief among them!

Witnessing such insane behavior made Marley rub her eyes in disbelief, but the madness would not disappear! "Why did I enlist with this pack of perverted pups?" she silently questioned. But before she could find an answer, Marley sensed an outside force and automatically pointed.

Thanks to Marley's warning, a pit bull and a pincher soon dragged a tall and slender hound into camp and took it straight to Bonaparte. As Marley moved closer to witness the captive's interrogation, she realized she knew this dog – it was Ivan of the First Mountain pack, her previous family! Ordered to bow and kiss the paw of Bonaparte, brave Ivan refused. When he would not respond to any questions, Bonaparte brought in a gargantuan, pug-faced boxer to teach Ivan a lesson. "Wham! Pow! Bam! Boom!" The boxer unleashed a series of powerful punches that sent Ivan into La La Land – he was out cold! Bonaparte ordered the unconscious Ivan caged, and the camp resumed its business.

The mistreatment of Ivan and the cats caused Marley to reflect on the insane behavior happening around her. And while doing so, she realized that the First Mountain pack was the sort of family she craved to be part of — not these lunatic Lost Dogs of Second Mountain.

"There are right things and wrong things in this world," Marley told herself, "and cats have just as much right to live as any animal. This army of Lost Dogs is on the wrong side of right, and I won't be part of it!"

As nightfall set in, and the camp became rowdier — dogs snarling and fighting, others ranting and raving and captive cats whining and moaning — Marley tiptoed over to Ivan.

"Ivan, Ivan, it's me, Marley. Are you alright? What are you doing here? How did you find me?" she whispered as she passed food and water through the cage bars.

"Hunter's excellent nose tracked you down, Marley, because the First Mountain pack wants to give you a second chance," explained Ivan. "We've devised an escape plan code-named Operation Free Marley — OFF-EM, for short — and here's what we have in mind."

After Ivan described plan OFF-EM to Marley, she unlocked his cage for a later escape, and then confessed to her errant ways.

"Ivan, you and the pack gave me a chance to experience the love of a good family, but I misbehaved and threw it away. To be honest, I was upset that Fritz might become a pack member before me, so I blamed the little guy and turned my anger on him. But the wild behavior of these Lost Dogs has quickly taught me right from wrong. And I now see that it's wrong to blame others for our problems like I blamed Fritz — like these mad dogs blame cats!"

Marley paused for a moment, as if deep in thought, and then posed a most serious question.

"I'm really sorry, Ivan, and I hope that the First Mountain pack can forgive me, someday. To make up for my wicked ways, I'd like to do what's right, and the right thing now is to free you and the cats. If I do some good, Ivan, will it atone for my mistreatment of Fritz?"

Ivan reached a paw through the cage, touched Marley on the cheek and responded with some kind words.

"Marley, it takes courage to admit our mistakes, strength to know right from wrong and bravery to stand up for the weak and defenseless. Since you now have those powers, I'm convinced that you'll make a fine addition to our pack. I'm not the smartest dog in the world, my friend, but I feel that a good deed is a giant step toward erasing a bad one. So, let's free the cats, make our escape and, if OFF-EM goes well, the pack will meet you at the bottom of First Mountain to welcome you home."

With that said, they added the final details to their daring escape plan, nuzzled farewell and then set Operation Free Marley in motion.

As the night wore on, and the wild creatures of Lost Dog camp settled in for some rest, Marley and Ivan implemented Phase I of OFF-EM. It began with Marley taking a position in the middle of the camp, so she could be easily seen by the sentinels. She then sent up a warning bark and went into pointing mode.

"Look! Look!" shouted a guard dog. "The black Lab's pointing at the main gate!"

The entire camp heard the alarm, sprang into action and ran to the main gate. With their attention diverted, Ivan slipped out of his cage, dashed to the captive cats and set them lose. "Live free and prosper!" he counseled as the cats fled out the back gate. "Live free and prosper!"

With the cats now liberated, Ivan crept along the camp perimeter toward the front entrance. As he did so, Marley made an about face – right on cue – and pointed to the empty cages near the back of the camp.

"Your Highness, the hound and the cats are gone!" cried a sentinel. And just as planned, all of the Lost Dogs rushed to the rear of the camp. By now, Ivan had snuck to the front entrance and, with perfect timing, Marley did a one-eighty and pointed out Ivan as he escaped through the unguarded gate.

"There's that disobedient mutt!" barked Bonaparte as Ivan fled the camp. "He deserves to be roasted alive and eaten for dinner! Sic him! Sic him, I say!"

On Bonaparte's command, the snarling camp dogs flew after Ivan, while Marley brought up the rear — just as called for in Phase I of Operation Free Marley.

As the Lost Dogs ran after their quarry, they were totally unaware that Phase II of OFF-EM was about to be deployed. Just out of sight of his pursuers, Ivan skirted the trail where the First Mountain pack had dug a sizable pit, camouflaged with branches and leaves. The vanguard of Bonaparte's wild dogs fell into the hidden trap and was taken out of action. But the rest of those vicious creatures avoided the trick and continued the chase. Marley was one of them — just as planned.

Now it was time for OFF-EM, Phase III to kick in. At a narrow point on the trail — bordered by a high wall on one side and a sheer drop-off on the other — Ivan's First Mountain mates engineered a series of taut ropes across the path. Agile Ivan knew the location of the snare and leapt over it, but many of the Lost Dogs were not as fortunate. Running at full tilt, they barreled into the ropes, got tripped up, tumbled over the cliff and out of the hunt. Nevertheless, some of those fierce beasts avoided the ambush and would not surrender. For them, Ivan's crew had prepared one more trap: Phase IV of Operation Free Marley was ready to go.

For Phase IV of OFF-EM to work, Marley needed to be at the head of Bonaparte's search party. As the Lost Dogs regrouped from the previous trap, Marley asked to be lead dog, so she could point out trouble before it happened. Thinking this a capital idea, those maniacs put Marley in front, but not until they swore an oath to capture Ivan and make a tasty stew of him!

After a considerable sprint down the trail, Marley found the spot where OFF-EM, Phase IV would happen. At this location, the trail narrowed and wound through a lengthy, steep-sided pass. It was here that Marley threw on the brakes and went into pointing mode. The pack skidded to a halt behind her, and Marley informed them that a trap had been laid up ahead.

"Let me investigate the trouble and I'll report back in a jiffy," offered Marley.

Permitted to proceed alone, Marley exited the pass, and Ivan and his mates sprang into action. Concealed above the corridor now filled with Lost Dogs, the First Mountain pack rolled boulders into both ends of the narrow passage and penned the fiends inside! OFF-EM, Phase IV had gone off without a hitch, and Marley rejoined her First Mountain mates along the trail.

The pack rejoiced at the sight of Marley. Fritz, Tuffy, Hunter, Josh, Kingston, and Ivan welcomed her back with intimate sniffs, warm nuzzles and high paws all around. But just as they thought they were home free, it happened – Marley went into pointing mode! And in no time at all, the pack heard the trouble Marley had sensed, for a most terrifying tune was carried to them by the wind:

One day, or another, we're gonna gitcha, we'll gitcha, we'll gitcha, gitcha, gitcha!

One way, or another, we'll gitcha, we'll gitcha, we'll gitcha, gitcha, gitcha!

"I know that song!" exclaimed a visibly shaken Marley. "Some Lost Dogs have gotten through the traps. Run for your lives!"

Pursued by the remnants of Bonaparte's army, the First Mountain pack ran as fast and as hard as their little legs would carry them. They scampered off Second Mountain and onto First Mountain trail, where they paused to catch their breath. But still they heard that eerie tune, and it was getting louder and louder, for the Lost Dogs were getting closer and closer!

We're gonna gitcha, we'll gitcha, we'll gitcha, gitcha, gitcha!

So, down the path they scurried, not stopping until they reached the safety of their homes, each dropping off the trail when they spotted their own house. Well, all the dogs except Marley, that is, for she was homeless and had no place to go!

Alone and fearing for her life, as the Lost Dogs moved closer for the kill, Marley saw one chance for survival and she took it. She spied a moving van, and its cargo door was open and the ramp was down. In search of safety, a frightened Marley tore into the trailer and squeezed behind some boxes. But in no time at all, the van door was closed and Marley was trapped inside. Confined in a small, dark space and hearing the loud noise of the big truck as it pulled away, Marley shivered with fear!

Awakened from her snooze on the deck by the appearance of Susan and Albert, Marley sprang to her feet, shook her entire body to regain her senses and ambled over to greet her family. As Albert scratched her head and Susan rubbed her haunches, Marley reveled in their attention.

"Aaah, friends and family, I'm so fortunate to have Susan and Albert as mine! They treat me to my favorite snacks, bread and pizza crusts – yum, yum! They take me for car rides and never scold me when I slobber on the windows – fun, fun! They take me for long walks and then shower me with affection – uh-hum, uh-hum! Am I the luckiest dog in the world, or what? Now, if I could just put an end to these Lost Dog nightmares, life would be a dream!"

Some tales are make-believe and some tales have actually happened. You can rest assured, dear reader, that everything in this tale is true – whether it happened or not.

Hannah Homes

And

Dr. Sprouty Walk

In . . .

THE CURIOUS
CASE OF THE
Hairless Hare

Story by **Clint Heverly**

Painting by **Denise Eileen Thurman**

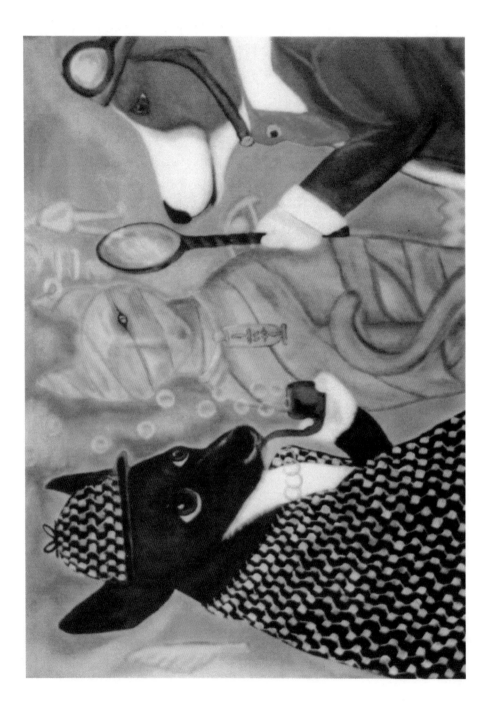

Some tales are make-believe and some tales have actually happened. You can rest assured, dear reader, that everything in this tale is true – whether it happened or not.

One's lifetime is filled with countless experiences and associations; most of which are unremarkable and some of which are best forgotten. But in my case, a special friendship and its accompanying adventure have spawned extraordinary moments for me. And so it was with the improbable incident I now make public for the first time – *The Curious Case of the Hairless Hare*.

This incredible adventure began on a steamy summer's day here in West Chester. I remember the day well, for Homes and I, undaunted by the excessive heat, had managed a rousing game of keepaway with her favorite toy – a squeaky lamb gifted by her grandmother. And, as usual, the famous canine sleuth had won the battle, since she is a splendid athlete. On the other hand, I would rather eat than exercise, so we followed our tug-of-war with breakfast on the veranda at #21 Rams Gate. Afterwards, at my insistence, Homes recounted her most recent case; one that I've aptly named *The Heart in a Jar Adventure*.

"The solution was elementary, my dear Dr. Walk," declared Homes with a serious look on her face, a mostly dark-haired face highlighted by a white chin. "For you see, old boy, most folks are not observant, not observant at all; they look, but they do not truly see. I, however, have trained to be a keen observer, and hence was able to find an explanation for the mysterious heart. But I must confess, old friend, that I could not have solved this riddle without your aid."

"What? What?" barked I, in total surprise of Homes' unwarranted praise. "I assisted in the solution? How so, Homes?"

"Unwittingly, dear doctor, but indeed you did. On the day I began my investigation of the puzzling heart, you shared an odd experience you'd had on a recent visit to an art museum. As you strolled through the galleries and admired the various works, your attention was captured by a most unusual painting; a painting whose purpose was to make the eye believe it was seeing one thing when, in fact, it was seeing another. You described this peculiar experience as an 'ocular confusion,' instead of the customary term 'optical illusion.' It was your misuse of words, doctor – which, I dare say, you may be unequalled at – that made me realize there was more to the grisly heart than first met the eye."

"As you may recall, Dr. Walk, this case concerned a freakishly large human heart, stored in a thick, green glass jar. The hideous object – kept as a curiosity by the town mortician, old man Chaplin – began to beat for no apparent reason. And according to the only witness – his son, Donald – the impossibility of a throbbing, disembodied heart had literally frightened the old man to death!"

"The bizarre and suspicious circumstances surrounding the undertaker's demise caused an inquiry by Inspector Hunter of the West Chester P.D. The inspector correctly surmised that old man Chaplin had indeed died of fright, for his face wore the unmistakable look of terror. But his investigation ground to a halt when the peculiar heart showed no apparent reason for its supposed supernatural activity."

"However, as I said before, doctor, folks look, but rarely do they see. And, ironically, the inspector is no exception! Unable to make headway in the case, Hunter asked for my assistance shortly after the old man was buried. And his timing was most fortunate, for your use of ocular confusion earlier that day had me thinking of the term optical illusion – a thought that was necessary to solve this puzzle."

"Yes, dear doctor, due to an optical illusion, created by the use of dense, green glass, the jar cleverly concealed a thicker than necessary bottom. But as I sought the purpose of this deception, misfortune reared her ugly head. For the inspector became so excited by my find that his wildly-wagging tail knocked the jar to the floor, and it shattered into a thousand pieces!"

"But as you well know, Dr. Walk, fortune is a fickle thing, and one's luck can change in an instant. With shards of glass everywhere, and the gigantic human heart lying at our feet, misfortune was quickly replaced by a stroke of good luck. For next to the grotesque organ lay a tiny, metallic gadget among the debris. The device, which had been hidden within the bogus base of the jar, turned out to be the machine which provided the motion and sound for the heart – 'thu-thump! thu-thump! thu-thump! thu-thump!' Now knowing that somebody had faked the killer heart, I confidently inferred that old man Chaplin was murdered – the vilest of sins!"

As I followed Homes' narrative, I couldn't help but admire the exceptional powers of reason this brindled Corgi possessed, for who would've thought that a 25 lb., wiry-haired dog could be so masterful at solving crime?

"When murder has been committed," continued Homes, "it is logical to hunt for the murderer and his motive close to the crime scene. That being the case, dear doctor, I had only to search as far as the deceased man's family to find both. Although the Chaplin family seemed to live a modest lifestyle, I discovered that the dead undertaker had amassed a fortune worth tens of millions of dollars."

"What? What?" questioned I, as I gulped down another bite of breakfast. "How could a funeral director acquire such great wealth? It does not make sense, Homes!"

"Precisely, Dr. Walk, how does a small town mortician become so wealthy? Because Donald stood to inherit his father's estate, I deduced that he was the murderer. And to prove it, I had only to turn the trick on the dead man's son — the very trick he used to kill his father."

"I duplicated the jarred heart, but added a slight twist, for I wanted Donald to believe that this heart was his father's very own. Not only did my replica throb and thump like the original, but a voice like his father's was added to cry out, 'Why did you kill me, Donald? Why did you frighten me to death?'"

"Our ruse now ready, the inspector and I scanned the local obituaries and learned that Donald would prepare his next cadaver for burial last night. We then snuck into the mortuary and hid our fabricated heart close to the fresh corpse. After making certain the apparatus worked, we took up a good viewing position behind a nearby louvered door."

"Not long after we'd set the trap, Donald entered the room and began the embalming process. And that's when Inspector Hunter put our heart into action. As you might imagine, doctor, the ghoulish sound of the throbbing heart — 'thu-thump! thu-thump! thu-thump! thu-thump!' — interspersed with a voice Donald thought to be his dead father's very own, nearly drove the lad to madness! Ironically, the boy became as pale as a corpse himself as he searched for the origin of the ghostlike voice and pounding heart!"

Homes then halted her fascinating account for a sip of water, a bite of biscuit and a toss of her stuffed hippo toy. But being engrossed in the tale and, therefore, impatient to hear the outcome, I finally shouted, "Come, come, Homes, out with it, old girl! Why would a son murder his father? What was his motive? What were his reasons?"

"The boy's motive was paradoxical, doctor, for his reasons were at once noble and ignoble. With our counterfeit heartbeat growing louder — 'thu-thump! thu-thump! thu-thump! thu-thump!' — and the dead man's simulated voice constantly crying, 'Why did you kill me, Donald? Why did you frighten me to death?' the lad was compelled to scream this confession:

'You know why I did it, you monster! You know why I killed you! I grew sick of breaking the laws of man and God! I grew tired of robbing the corpses – the rings from their fingers, the jewelry from their wrists and necks, the gold from their teeth! Your greed still not satisfied, you forced me to harvest body parts, too, you old devil! And what were you doing with our ill-gotten gains? Nothing, you miser, nothing at all! You were just watching the wealth accumulate! Well, not me, father, not me! I'm going to spend it! Do you hear me, father? I'm going to spend it!'"

"With Donald now totally unglued, the inspector and I leapt from our blind, and the rest is history, as they say."

Her tale now over, Homes stood on her hind legs, pumped her white-socked paws into the air above her head and pirouetted around the veranda on her tippy-toes. She calls this performance her "victory dance" – an act that some think is caused by an inflated ego. But I know better, for Hannah is the humblest of dogs. Finished with her dance, Homes began to unwind by chewing her squeaky hippo toy, whence I began to praise her excellent detective skills.

"Bravo, Hannah Homes! Another superb job of solving an un-solvable crime! I'm recording your deeds and I'll make them known someday. If you weren't so modest, old girl, I believe the world could be your clam!"

With that, Homes rolled her eyes, shook her head in exasperation and then gently corrected me by saying, "That's 'oyster,' Sprouty. You mean to say 'the world could be your oyster.'"

I was about to protest Homes' castigation of my misstated maxim, but she suddenly barked out a most intriguing announcement: "A hare with long, floppy ears is about to enter our lives, my friend!"

And just as Homes had finished her improbable prediction, a large brown and white hare appeared on our porch – making her prophecy as astounding as a magician pulling a rabbit from a hat! The hare was somewhat mangy-looking and possessed the longest ears

I'd ever seen, for they dragged on the floor as he lethargically moved forward. Seeming exhausted and breathing heavily, the visitor gave us a quizzical look and then asked, in the saddest of voices, "Which of you is Madam Homes?" To cheer the poor fellow, I wanted to say that all he need do is peek under our tails. But I did not get the opportunity to make the joke, for our guest promptly launched into an explanation of his unusual name, followed by a tale of woe.

"Let me begin by telling you that my name is Rab-Bit — that's spelled r,a,b,-,b,i,t — not r,a,b,b,i,t as most would think. You see, when hare's wed, they combine their first names to form a new last name. In my case, Rab joined with Bit. The jointure necessitates the use of a hyphen and that changes pronunciation. As a result, my name is pronounced Rab-Bit, not rabbit. Next to his health, a hare's married name and his reputation are his most precious possessions, and they mustn't be dishonored."

"Be that as it may, Mrs. Rab-Bit and I are the curators of the museum here in town. Well, we were in charge until this past Saturday. Due to a tragic incident, we have since been demoted and hence face disgrace. To make matters worse, we have also become extremely ill. My wife has grown wan and nearly hairless. And, as you can readily see, I, too, have begun losing my hair and health. We have been examined by the best physicians in town, but none can find an explanation for our sickness. And that's why I'm here. I'm told that Hannah Homes is the only one who can save us from certain death!"

"I'm a doctor," said I to Rab-Bit, "but I fail to see how Madam Homes — who is not a physician — can cure your illness."

With that, I thought the hare would faint to the floor, for he turned ashen and weak-kneed. Homes spit out her chew toy, jumped to her feet and helped the hare to a comfortable lounge chair. As the miserable fellow lay there gasping for air, I massaged the bridge of his nose — a treatment I learned in veterinarian school. In short order, our caller regained his composure, and that's when Homes introduced us.

"I am Hannah Walk Homes and, unlike my colleague here, Dr. Sprouty Walk, I think I know why you require our assistance, Mr. Rab-Bit. Let's see if I'm right, sir. First, isn't it true that some rare and valuable artifacts have gone missing – objects that were under your care and supervision?"

The hare nodded in the affirmative and Homes continued her questioning.

"And isn't it true that you and Mrs. Rab-Bit suffer from strange ailments caused by a curse – a curse you think I can break?"

Again, much to my astonishment, the hare vigorously nodded "yes," causing his extra long ears to flop up and down and slap comically against the floor.

"And isn't it true that the missing items are, in fact, Egyptian mummies?"

After the last of Homes' prescient questions, the hare sprang from the chair and, with an expression of great joy on his white face, shot straight at Homes. He then gave Hannah what I call a "bunny hug," for he shoved his head into her lap and rubbed his muzzle against her belly for about 30 seconds! After his extraordinary display of emotion, the hare explained the cause of his obvious delight.

"You have just demonstrated your amazing powers of detection, Madam Homes, and I am convinced that you are the Rab-Bits' last chance for survival. Please, Madam Homes, please agree to help us!"

After the hare's pathetic plea for assistance, Homes began chewing her stuffed sheep toy – something that helps her think through a problem. A few moments later, she tossed the toy over her shoulder, looked the sickly hare straight in the eye and said, "I sympathize with your plight, Mr. Rab-Bit, but I need more facts before I consent to solve this peculiar mystery. You must tell me all you know, starting at the beginning."

With this request from Homes, the hare resumed his curious tale, while Hannah continued to chew her stuffed sheep.

"We Rab-Bits have studied ancient mummification techniques for many years, and that's why we were hired as museum curators. For, you see, Madam Homes, the museum had recently acquired a collection of Egyptian mummies, and it wanted to learn all it could of the curiosities before putting them on display."

It was at this point in the hare's story that Homes interrupted with her first of several penetrating questions.

"Sir, what is the nature of the mummies, and how did they go missing?"

"Oddly enough, Madam Homes, there were no humans among the lot, only animal mummies. There was a crocodile, a leopard, a serpent and a falcon. We had been examining them for a week or so when disaster struck late last Friday. During our research that evening, we became inexplicably exhausted and were forced to break for a nap. When we awoke, the falcon and the leopard were gone!"

"So, Mr. Rab-Bit," interrupted Homes, "what action did you take when you found that the mummies were missing?"

"We notified Inspector Hunter of the West Chester P.D. as quickly as we could, Madam Homes. Hunter, who looks much like Doctor Walk, is a brown and white Beagle with the nose of a bloodhound. He conducted an immediate and thorough search, but to no avail, for the mummies had vanished, as if into thin air. However, the inspector did manage to sniff out several clues, and he has graciously allowed me to share them with you."

Hearing the word "clues" made Hannah's ears snap to attention, and she started to scratch behind her left one — something she involuntarily does when excited by the possibility of adventure. She told the hare she was well acquainted with Inspector Hunter, and then she eagerly posed her next question: "What are those clues, sir? Please be as thorough and as detailed as possible."

"The most obvious piece of evidence," replied the hare, "was a metal gurney parked next to the North Exit, not far from the laboratory where we last saw the mummies. Inspector Hunter said the gurney was used to transport the missing mummies from the lab to the exit, where they were then removed from the museum. However, no alarm sounded, and the monitor has no record of an open door. What do you make of that, Madam Homes?"

"I have some thoughts, Mr. Rab-Bit, but first I must know the other clues found by the inspector. I imagine you studied the mummies in a sterile setting. Was anything unusual found there? Were there any extraordinary prints, for example?"

"As you say, Madam Homes, the examination room is a glass-enclosed, sterile environment. Inspector Hunter dusted for prints, but none were found except for ours, and, of course, those of our occasional assistant, Mr. Katt."

"Hmmm, that is odd, odd indeed," offered Homes while gnawing on her stuffed sheep – a habit of hers as she ponders a problem. "But you said there were several possible clues, Mr. Rab-Bit. What else was found at the crime scene?"

The hare reached into a pouch dangling from his waist and produced a feather found in the examination room. He handed it to Homes, who passed it to me and asked if I knew the bird of origin.

"Hawk of some sort," proffered I, "possibly a falcon. But how could a feather have anything to do with this mystery, Homes?"

"Have patience, dear doctor, for we shall know the feather's significance in due course. Now, Mr. Rab-Bit, what other evidence do you have for us?"

The hare reached into his pouch and gingerly extracted a scrap of linen-like paper. The paper looked most ancient and was covered with exquisitely crafted symbols which Homes immediately identified as hieroglyphics – a form of picture writing used by the priests of ancient Egypt.

"Yes! Yes!" exclaimed the hare. "The writing is Egyptian hiero-glyphics, Madam Homes. It was found by Inspector Hunter near the gurney at the North Exit."

The hare then produced a translation of the glyphs which he read to us:

Hail ye gods who make the soul enter into the body.
May my soul gaze upon my earthly body.
May my soul take up its abode in my body.
May it neither perish nor be destroyed.
May my soul live for ever and ever.

"Oddly enough, Madam Homes, we Rab-Bits, with the aid of Mr. Katt, discovered this piece of hieroglyphic writing beneath the wrappings of the falcon mummy. How it ended up on the floor by the North Exit is a mystery to us!"

The hare handed his translation to Homes. She eyed it briefly, passed it to me and then asked her next question.

"Do I understand correctly, Mr. Rab-Bit, that the fragment of hieroglyphic writing you hold in your paw is the very one your team discovered as you unwrapped the falcon mummy?"

The hare nodded in the affirmative, and that prompted Homes' next question.

"Can you shed any light on its purpose, sir?"

"Mrs. Rab-Bit – bless her sickly heart – reads hieroglyphs as well as any expert and hence is certain of two things. First of all, these symbols represent an incantation, a magic spell of sorts. Secondly, this incantation can be seen in the tomb of Tutankhamen, the pharaoh most of us know as King Tut."

The thought of his ill wife caused the hare to violently sob again. But Homes allayed his fears by saying, "I have some solid ideas on solving this mystery, Mr. Rab-Bit, especially since we know that these glyphs have magical power. However, it is imperative that you con-tinue your tale, so please tell me about the curse."

"Ah, the unfortunate curse," said the hare, somewhat ruefully. "It has become the bane of our existence, just as a curse was for the discoverers of Tut's tomb – the ones who mysteriously died shortly thereafter. The curse originated with our examination of the bird mummy. The mummy was that of a raptor – a falcon, to be precise – contained in a wonderful wooden box, adorned with beautiful hieroglyphs. My wife's translation of the writing revealed this curse:

Death comes on wings to he who opens this sacred sarcophagus."

"As you probably know from your medical training, Dr. Walk, we hares are highly prone to superstition, so the curse frightened us immensely. But we are strongly driven to perform our duties, too, so we sloughed it off and continued our work. However, much to our dismay, we encountered another curse inside the coffin:

They who violate my mummy shall suffer a fire inside, a loss of hair, and be cooked with the damned."

"The second curse has turned out to be most prophetic, Madam Homes. As you can readily see from my mangy coat, we Rab-Bits have suffered mightily from its wrath – especially my dear wife who has become virtually hairless! Do you have any idea how important a sleek and well-coiffed fur coat is to a hare, Madam Homes?"

With that, the poor fellow began to weep, so I rubbed his nose until his tears subsided, whence Hannah continued her interrogation.

"Tell me about the fever and your hair loss," said Homes. "When did they first occur?"

"The loss of hair and the fever-like symptoms began shortly after we encountered the curses, Madam Homes. As I stated before, our work on the mummies was inexplicably tiring, so we often required a nap to refresh ourselves. As we groggily awoke from our naps, we always had the same hallucination – the shadow of a falcon-like bird would appear on the wall for a few seconds. Then the shadow would disappear and our innards would begin to burn – as if on fire.

And, worst of all, we would find that we were missing more hair. Speaking of hair, that's another thing Inspector Hunter found at the crime scene — a clump of hair. Well, actually, it's fur — rabbit fur, to be precise."

The hare produced a sizable clump of brown fur from his pouch, passed it to us and then continued his narrative.

"The fur appears to be either mine or my wife's, as we Rab-Bits are the same color. It was found by Inspector Hunter on the metal gurney — the gurney he says the culprits used to transport the mummies from the museum. But I swear to you, Madam Homes and Dr. Walk, we Rab-Bits were never near that gurney, so how could the fur be ours? And if it is ours, how did it end up on the gurney?"

The hare's oath sounded most sincere to Homes and me, so we assured the poor fellow that we trusted the truthfulness of his tale. Then Homes asked, "Is there any other possible evidence, Mr. Rab-Bit? Have you covered everything?"

"The inspector found this mysterious item in the examination room wastebasket," said the hare as he reached into his pouch to retrieve a piece of paper with strange symbols on it. He handed it to Homes who pondered it at great length. She then passed it to me and asked what I made of it. It appeared to be some form of writing, but it baffled my senses so greatly that I could not make heads or tails of it! I handed the incomprehensible thing back to Homes, confessed to total confusion and asked for her judgment.

"I believe it to be a cipher, a coded message," explained Homes, "but let us analyze it at a later time. Now, Mr. Rab-Bit, I have one final question for you. Who is managing the museum since you have been replaced?"

"A very learned cat of Egyptian origin and pedigree has assumed the role of curator, Madam Homes. His name is Kitt E. Katt and he is well respected amongst our circle of Egyptologists. It appears that Mr. Katt was part of a package deal with the unknown donor of the mummies: if the museum wanted the mummies, then Katt came with them. Luckily, Katt has great expertise in our field, and he has been quite valuable to our research. The museum is fortunate to have such an eminent scientist take our place."

Homes scratched behind her left ear and then behind the right – a reflexive action she performs as she arrives at a decision. Then she looked the hare straight in the eye and said, "You are in a pickle, Mr. Rab-Bit, and you'll only get out of it with my help. So, let's meet at your museum today at one p.m. for a tour of the crime scene."

With Homes' acceptance of the case, the re-energized hare flew across the porch and locked her in a bunny hug. Then, much to my chagrin – for I detest physical contact unless I initiate it – the hare bounded over to me and duplicated his hug, pressing his nose into my tummy and rubbing it wildly against my flesh! As I pushed him away in disgust, the overly demonstrative hare gleefully gushed, "Thank you, thank you, Dr. Walk and Madam Homes! I'm starting to feel better already! See you at one o'clock sharp." The hare then skipped across the veranda, bounced down the stairs and jauntily hopped along the sidewalk toward the museum – acting like he had just experienced a miraculous cure!

"So, dear doctor, what do you make of the hare's curious tale?" queried Homes as Rab-Bit passed out of sight.

So astonished was I by the hare's unusual account and Homes' show of remarkable reasoning power – not to mention the hare's unwanted affection – that I was momentarily stunned into silence! But, in due time, I regained my senses and managed to ask, "I know you are an amazing detective, Hannah, but how in the world were you able to foretell the hare's difficult situation?"

"Ha!" snapped Homes. "The facts were there for the taking, old boy; facts that allowed me to know the hare's problems beforehand, just as I know that you did not read the Sunday paper. Do you possess a copy, sir?"

Flabbergasted that Homes somehow knew I had not read the Sunday newspaper, I meekly answered that I did have a copy, which I quickly fetched. As I unfolded it to the front page, an item relevant to this mystery immediately grabbed my attention:

Mummies Go Missing From Local Museum

It was announced Saturday morning by Inspector Hunter of the West Chester P.D. that two ancient Egyptian mummies recently acquired by the West Chester Museum – the mummies of a leopard and a falcon – may have been purloined. The museum curators, Mr. and Mrs. Rab-Bit, have been relieved of their directorships until the issue is resolved. When questioned by this reporter, Mr. Rab-Bit refused to discuss the matter citing a severe illness in his family that required his immediate attention. The renowned Inspector Hunter will lead the investigation into the disappearance of the rare and valuable artifacts. Hunter declined to provide any further information regarding the crime, but he characteristically predicted an early resolution to the case. Meanwhile, a recent hire at the museum, Mr. Kitt E. Katt, has been named acting curator.

"Well, Homes, I now see how you obtained foreknowledge of the hare and his mummies," said I, after reading the news account, "but how on Earth did you know of the curse?"

"Aha, dear doctor, the curse was the least problematic prediction of all, for no reputable mummy has ever been laid to rest without one!"

And with that, Homes fell onto her back, extended her white-tipped paws skyward and pumped her legs as if riding a bicycle – something she always does when amused by her own words. After what I thought to be a rather weak attempt at humor, Hannah quickly returned to her usual sober self.

"I simply put two and two together, old friend, to foretell the hare's predicament. And based on Rab-Bit's responses to my examination, I anticipate an exciting adventure. How about you, Doctor

Walk? Are you willing to assist in my quest to solve the mystery of the missing mummies, and thereby help the hare regain his health and good name?"

Awed by Homes' supreme powers of reason, and wanting to see more of dogdom's most brilliant detective in action, I consented to lend a paw to the investigation. Then I bravely added, "I don't think the hare is cursed, Homes, for I do not believe in the supernatural. Do you?"

Tossing her chew toy aside and shrugging her shoulders, Homes equivocated by saying, "I'm not sure, Sprouty, I'm just not sure. Did you know that Lord Carnarvon, financial backer for the excavation of King Tut's tomb, died at the very hour Howard Carter opened the burial site? A curse at the entrance to Tut's tomb had promised as much. Was Carnarvon's death mere co-incidence, sir?"

"Be that as it may, Homes, I for one am certain there are no curses in this world. Just as I am certain that we should begin our investigation A.S.A.P., for a stitch in time saves crime."

Hearing another botched adage on my part, Homes jumped to her feet, shook her head from side-to-side to show her irritation and said, "A stitch in time saves nine! I repeat, doctor, a stitch in time saves nine! Whatever will we do with you, my friend?"

With Homes attired in her signature black and white houndstooth cape, and I outfitted in my biking helmet with attached goggles, we dismounted my bicycle at precisely one p.m. and entered the museum. We asked for Mr. Rab-Bit, but were ushered into the new curator's office, instead. And once inside, I immediately began to drool, for I detected the unmistakable aroma of one of my all-time favorite foods – chocolate chip cookies!

"I am Kitt E. Katt, museum curator," announced a stunningly handsome cat that had been licking its foot. The fastidious feline politely stopped grooming himself and extended a freshly cleaned paw to both of us. His appearance was quite striking, for he was long, tall and slender and he possessed an amazing coat of silky, golden fur, dotted with many black spots. In short, he looked more like a miniature leopard than a domesticated puss. With smugness in his voice that, I dare say, only a dog could detect, Mr. Katt then offered, "Am I to understand that you wish to see the Rab-Bits? You do know they have been temporarily removed from their duties pending the outcome of the mummy mystery, do you not?"

At this point, Homes introduced us, explained our presence and offered our services to the investigation.

"Ah, Madam Homes," purred the cat, "your reputation and that of your able assistant, Dr. Walk, precede you. However, I must inform you that Inspector Hunter has finished his inquiry and intends to make an arrest by tomorrow. Therefore, I fear your offer to assist the investigation is a little too late."

I sensed that the new curator was giving us the brush-off, and was about to register a protest when Homes announced, "Well, Mr. Katt, since you have no need of our services, then we shall be going. Do have a good day, sir. And good day to you, too, Mr. Bird," added Homes as she reached out to stroke a most decrepit and unusual looking fellow sitting near Kitt E. Katt's desk. The bird, which appeared to be a hybrid of some sort, was perched atop a T-shaped post, and was surrounded by several mirrors which dangled from the ceiling.

"The parrot's name is Horus, but he cannot hear you, Madam Homes," explained the cat. "He seldom speaks anymore, does not fly well and can barely see, either. In short, Horus is quite old, and hence has lost most of his faculties. Unfortunately, chocolate chip cookies are one of the few pleasures he has left in life. Would you like to feed him a cookie, Dr. Walk?"

The cat handed me a bag of beautifully browned discs, loaded with scrumptious looking chocolate bits — the very same treats I'd been lusting for since entering his office! I took three; one for the bird and, of course, two for myself. I devoured my two in one fell swoop, whilst the parrot weakly nibbled his as he perched amongst the mirrors. After we watched the broken-down fellow consume the cookie — which took quite some time due to his extreme old age — Homes repeated our departure.

"Well, since I cannot talk with the parrot, Mr. Katt, perhaps I will have better luck conversing with the Rab-Bits."

"I am afraid that will be impossible, Madam Homes," retorted the cat, "for they are napping in a back room and wish not to be disturbed."

"Now see here, Mr. Katt!" snapped I, miffed that we were again turned away from our investigation. But I could not continue my protest, for Homes abruptly cut me off and nudged me toward the door, causing me to miss a grab for another cookie as we departed. Down the corridor we trotted as quickly as our little legs would carry us. Out the front door and down the steps we flew to my bicycle. I pedaled fast and furiously, and we did not speak until we stopped at the town square, whence Homes opened with the phrase she always uses when feeling the challenge of the hunt.

"By Jove, Dr. Walk, the game is now afoot! It is mere supposition at this point, doctor, but I believe the cat and parrot are at the center of this mystery!"

"The parrot?" asked I, confused by Hannah's prediction. "Why, the old bird is barely alive, Homes! On what do you base your unreasonable theory?"

"A linguistic lapse on your part, doctor, has caused me to jump to an irrational conclusion. Just a few days ago you confidently declared that 'a zebra cannot change its spots.' But you should have said 'a leopard cannot change its spots,' or 'a zebra cannot change its stripes.' These are oft-used adages, doctor, but they do not always hold true. For I guarantee that we shall see two animals literally change their appearance before this thing is over!"

After making her puzzling prediction, Homes scratched behind her left ear and then behind the right — as she is wont to do when arriving at a decision — and then laid out the following agenda.

"I know you're famished, dear doctor, so here's my plan. You will go home to lunch, and to study the coded message. Meanwhile, I shall search the library for information on our suspects, Katt and Horus. I'll see you at the dinner hour, sir."

And with her cape waving wonderfully behind her, Hannah sprinted off to the library. Then I mounted my bicycle and pedaled to #21 Rams Gate to mix business with pleasure — to snack while pondering the cipher.

Several hours passed and, just as planned, Homes returned to Rams Gate around six p.m., and immediately asked what I had made of the coded message.

"Why, Homes, I cannot make heads or tails of it!" groused I, frustration showing in my voice. "I've devoted hours to the task, but the writing consistently appears *bassackwards* to my senses!"

"Did you say *bassackwards*, Sprouty? Don't you mean to say *assbackwards*?" questioned Homes, with a hint of aggravation in her voice. But her irritation caused by my misuse of words soon turned to joy, for in no time at all she shouted, "Why, Dr. Walk, you clever dog, you've done it again! Your verbal blunder has provided the key to the cipher. Don't you see, old boy, the words on the paper are indeed *bassackwards*. Bring me a mirror and I'll prove it."

I fetched a hand mirror and Homes held the message to it. The mirrored image looked like this:

harehasincantationretrieveforrceremonylastchancefading-fastmeetin0at2300h

Hannah then copied the cipher's reflection and put some breaks at appropriate places. And, like magic, the following message appeared:

hare has incantation   retrieve for r ceremony   last chance fading fast   meet in 0 at 2300 h

"By Jove, doctor, thanks to your outstanding work on the cipher, along with my successful trip to the library, we are well on our way to solving this mummy mystery!" gushed Homes.

And with that, she performed a victory dance to show her delight. With her white-tipped forepaws held high above her head, she stood on her tippy-toes and twirled about the veranda like a whirling dervish. Frankly, I thought her dance was premature, for I was not as optimistic as she. So, I did not hesitate to speak my mind.

"Hannah, although I can read the words, I cannot understand their meaning. What *incantation*? What *ceremony*? What do the cryptic terms *r*, *fading fast*, *0, 2300* and *h* indicate?"

"Have patience, good doctor," advised Homes. "With a bit more research on our part, all will soon be revealed. Now, let's put our mystery on hold and eat some supper. Mrs. Henderson has prepared your favorite dish this evening — Welsh rarebit. Afterwards, it's off to bed, since tomorrow promises to be a long day, old friend."

After a quick breakfast the next morning — a breakfast far too speedy for me, for I enjoy my food more than most — Homes made an astonishing claim.

"If my thinking is correct, doctor, the mummies are still in the museum. So, we must do some snooping there as soon as possible."

Off to the museum we went, Hannah trotting for exercise and I riding my bike. Upon arrival, Homes set us straight to our first task, measuring the circumference of the two hundred year old building. It was a chore made easy, because Homes and I have long realized that each one of my natural steps is precisely one foot in length. Our perambulation of the stately structure soon yielded its dimensions; it was 240 feet by 240 feet, a perfect square.

We then ascended the steps to the front door, but, as luck would have it, the museum was closed to the public this day. However, with a little probing on our part, we located an unlocked and unguarded service entrance that gave us access to the bottom floor — the place where the mummies were last seen, and where I would witness Hannah's brilliant mind in action, yet again.

Once inside, our reconnaissance of the basement was greatly aided by a museum brochure. There were six rooms on this level, numbered 01 through 06. Rooms 01 through 05 were artifact display galleries. The Examination/Restoration Laboratory – the room where the Rab-Bits last saw the missing mummies – was labeled 06. Three rooms were on the east side of the building and three on the west side, the two sides being separated by a spacious corridor. There were emergency exits at either end of the hallway: one exit faced south, while the other opened to the north. It was near the stairs to the North Exit that Inspector Hunter found the gurney and the clump of rabbit hair.

Having learned the layout of the floor, we began a methodical investigation to find the dimensions of every room. We measured each gallery by counting my steps, one to a foot, and Homes scribbled furiously on her notepad as we went. Occasionally she would call a halt to our exploration and chew on her stuffed sheep – a certain indication that an important conclusion was near at hand. Once our measurements were completed, Homes did some rapid calculations, and then drew a rudimentary map of the floor. We studied the diagram for a good five minutes before she exuberantly declared, "By Jupiter, Dr. Walk, I think we're onto something here! Did you notice anything odd concerning the room numbers?"

"I find it strange," said I, "that each room number begins with a zero. Why are they numbered 01, 02, etc.? What do you make of that, Homes?"

"Bravo, Doctor Walk!" cried Homes. "A keen observation on your part, sir, for I believe the numbering scheme to be a significant clue. Since the coded message reads *'meet in 0 at 2300 h,'* I'm convinced there's another room down here, doctor – a hidden room designated *'0.'*"

Homes made a few more calculations on her pad, and then en-thusiastically shouted, "Follow me, doctor!" We darted down the corridor to the north side of the building where Homes had me re-measure the two galleries at that end. Then, swift as lightening, we flew to the south end of the floor and repeated our measurements. A few moments passed and then Homes made another surprising announcement.

"If our measurements are correct, doctor, a space of three feet is unaccounted for on the north side of the building. The interiors of the two galleries on the south end total 210 feet in length, while the two on the north side add to 207. If everything else is equal – the thickness of the walls, the width of the hallway, etc. – then three feet of interior space is missing on the north end of building! How does three feet of space disappear, Dr. Walk? Where does it go?"

Homes reworked her calculations and reviewed her map. And, in no time all, she yelped, "Follow me, doctor, and I will show you the missing footage!"

Off we raced to the area beneath the North Exit staircase, the place where Inspector Hunter had found the gurney and the rabbit hair. No sooner had we arrived than the strangest sensation struck me, and I was compelled to blurt out, "Homes, it must be approaching lunch hour, for I detect the delicious aroma of chocolate chip cookies!"

Because we had eaten just a short while ago, Homes shot me a look of scorn. But she soon changed her tune and asked, "What's that, Dr. Walk? You smell chocolate chip cookies? Where's the scent coming from, old boy?"

My nose set straight to work and, in short order, I reported a most puzzling find. The source of the delectable scent of chocolate chip cookies originated *behind* the nearby wall! Homes reached into her hound's-tooth cape, retrieved a magnifying glass and inspected the wall panel. Then she used her expert paws to apply sideways pressure and, amazingly, the partition began to move! And as the panel slid open, it revealed a descending staircase. Ta-da! It was the missing three feet!

Nonplussed by her discovery of a secret entrance – for she knew she would find one – Homes reached into her cape and produced a small flashlight. She entered the dark space and I gladly followed in hopes of finding cookies. We carefully worked our way down a flight of narrow steps and entered a sizable cavern beneath the basement floor. After Homes lit some candles, and our eyes grew accustomed to the soft light, we fully expected to see the mummies. But, to our dismay, there were none! As a matter of fact, the only objects in the room were velvet curtains covering each wall and three small platforms arranged like a staircase.

Homes asked me to stand in place while she searched for evidence. She sniffed behind the curtains and around the platforms, but to no avail. Next, she inspected the floor and found the only clue in the room – a half-eaten chocolate chip cookie. Homes held the cookie to her flashlight beam for close scrutiny. Afterwards, she presented the treat to me for my analysis and, of course, eventual consumption. With her examination now finished, she made an astounding declaration.

"Well, well, well, Dr. Walk, your nose knows, eh, old boy? Thanks to your insatiable craving for chocolate, I am now convinced of two things. Firstly, this cavern is the room designated '0' in the coded message. Secondly, if we're in this secret room no later than 10:30 tonight, our investigation will come to a most remarkable and rewarding end. It is now five p.m. and the dinner hour beckons, so let's return to Rams Gate and grab a bite to eat. Afterwards, we'll track down Inspector Hunter and invite him to tonight's fireworks."

After a dinner of succulent leftovers – which I sinfully chased with a generous portion of pie-ala-mode – we met Inspector Hunter and informed him of the secret room beneath the museum.

"So, Madam Homes, you've located a heretofore unknown room below the basement," barked a self-assured Inspector Hunter, "but since it holds no mummies, I fail to see what bearing your discovery has on this case. We already know who stole the mummies and we intend to make an arrest. Then it's just a matter of time before we know the whole truth, for I guarantee that the culprits will sing like a chorus of crows once we have them in custody."

"And who might the guilty party be, my dear inspector?" asked Homes with an obvious smirk on her face and a telling disdain in her voice.

"An easy answer, Madam Homes!" snorted the inspector. "It was the Rab-Bits. They were the last to handle the mummies, and rabbit hair was found on the gurney they used to spirit their prize from the museum."

"What about the alarm, Inspector Hunter? Why didn't it sound if the exit door was used to remove the mummies from the museum?"

The best the inspector could do to answer Hannah's piercing question was to lamely state, "The system must have a glitch, Homes. It is plain to see that the North Exit was used to steal the mummies. Since the alarm did not sound, there must have been a malfunction. What else could it be?"

"Why, Inspector Hunter, you disappoint me, old boy!" chastised Homes. "We've worked together on numerous cases, and I've never heard you offer a flimsier theory!"

Then Homes delivered her *coup de grace* of questions.

"And the Rab-Bits' motive, Inspector Hunter? What in the world could it be, sir?"

Without batting an eye, the inspector proudly announced his premise.

"Mummia, Homes, finely ground mummy. You are aware of the purported powers of ground mummy, are you not, madam? Why you, Dr. Walk, you're a physician. You've studied the mummia phenomenon, have you not, sir?"

I nodded a "yes" to Hunter's question, and then promptly rattled off the first stanza of Rupert Brooke's poem, *Mummia*:

As those of old drank mummia
To fire their limbs of lead.
Making dead kings from Africa
Stand pandar to their bed.

I wanted to continue, but Hannah struck first:

Drunk on the dead, and medicined
With spiced imperial dust,
In a short night they reeled to find
Ten centuries of lust.

"Alright! Alright!" interrupted a ruffled Inspector Hunter before we could finish our recitation. "It's obvious you two are well acquainted with mummia, so you should certainly understand why the Rab-Bits wanted the mummies for their own. As the poem tells us, ground mummy is used as both a love potion and a Fountain of Youth drug, and there are many who would pay top dollar for a tiny taste of it. I rest my case, Homes, for two plus two will always equal four!"

Hannah leaned back on her haunches and extended her left forepaw toward Hunter — a posture she often assumes when about to disagree. Then she lambasted the officer for a theory that sounded more like pure speculation than solid reason.

"So, my dear inspector, you're about to arrest the Rab-Bits based on scant, circumstantial evidence and a hunch about drug dealing. Oh, Hunter, my Hunter! You are so far from the truth that you may never find it without our assistance!"

"Oh, is that so, Homes!" snapped the indignant officer. "If you're so smart, what's your solution?"

"Accompany Dr. Walk and me this evening," said a confident Homes, "and I guarantee that all will be revealed. Not only will we find the mummies, we shall see who stole them and learn their motive for doing so, as well."

The inspector was skeptical of our claim, but reluctantly agreed to join us.

"I believe you two are barking up the wrong tree, Madam Homes. However, we Beagles are a proud breed and, as I am sure Dr. Walk well knows, we are born to seek the truth, wherever that may lead us and no matter how we arrive there. Count me in, Homes."

As stealthily as possible, we entered the museum basement that special Thursday evening and descended into the hidden cavity below the floor – Homes leading the way, guided by her flashlight beam. Once inside the secret room, Inspector Hunter barked in amazement, "Why, this looks like a stop on the Underground Railroad, Dr. Walk, a safe haven for escaped slaves on their journey to freedom! Such hiding places were provided by anti-slavery Quakers, and there are many beneath the oldest buildings of our town. How on earth did you find this place, Homes?"

"It's a long story, inspector, one that I promise to tell you someday. But right now we must hide behind this curtain, for our evidence suggests that a unique and amazing spectacle will begin at *'2300 h'* – a time that fast approaches."

We slipped behind the curtain, but we three dogs had great difficultly secreting ourselves due to our extreme excitement. Our tongues panted rapidly and our tails wagged wildly, causing the curtain to shimmer and shake as if it had a life of its own! Finally, after much admonishing of one another, we were able to will our rear appendages and panting tongues to a halt. And it was none too soon, for as 11 p.m. arrived, Homes detected some extraneous sounds unheard by neither the inspector nor me. "Hush now," she cautioned, "somebody approaches!"

Shortly thereafter we heard footfalls and fluttering, accompanied by a bright beam of light. Our hearts raced wildly as we caught our first glimpse of the perpetrators and, once again, Homes was prescient. For as candles were lit by our suspects, we could see that Kitt E. Katt and Horus had entered the room! The duo said nary a word, but set straight to their tasks of removing the mummies from a hidden vault in the wall, and then laying them out on the middle of the three platforms — heads facing east. Next, they placed what appeared to be a large crystal ball on the lowest platform. The leopard-like cat then scampered to the uppermost shelf and the bird — now looking surprisingly more like a falcon than a parrot — flew to meet him.

It was at this point that Inspector Hunter almost ruined our surveillance, for his instincts urged him to rush the pair and arrest them on the spot! However, Homes managed to restrain the eager Beagle, and persuaded him to hold off so that we could learn their motive. And how fortuitous, for we then witnessed not a criminal act, but a most incredible event — one that was both awe-inspiring and amazingly beautiful!

As Kitt E. Katt and Horus assumed their positions on the highest platform, an ancient religious rite unfolded before our eyes. It started as the cat and bird chanted a petition to Osiris, the Egyptian god of death, proclaiming they had led a life of innocence:

We have not dishonored our family. We have not caused pain and suffering. We have not murdered. We are pure. We are pure. We are pure.

The bird — now looking *exactly* like a falcon — continued the petition with a prayer of his own:

O, great Isis, wife of our lord Osiris, hear my prayer.
My falcon soul has been trapped outside my mummy lo these 85 years.
Help my soul reunite with my mummy.
Help my soul rejoin my family that we may live in bliss and harmony for ever and ever.

The cat then handed the bird a scrap of paper from which Horus recited his final prayer – a prayer Homes and I recognized as the same one Mr. Rab-Bit had shown us yesterday:

Hail ye gods who make the soul enter into the body.
May my soul take up its abode in my body.
May it neither perish nor be destroyed.
May my soul live for ever and ever.

The bird, now finished with his prayers, lay down on the platform, head pointing eastward. Then Kitt E. Katt took up the ceremony with words that sounded as soft and sweet as the purring of a contented puss. He asked Osiris to allow his soul to leave his cat body and take up its rightful place in the leopard mummy – to dwell there for eternity. Once finished with his prayer, the magnificently-spotted cat lay beside the bird and together they continued to chant their magical incantations. Yes, magical words, I say, for that is precisely what they turned out to be!

As the song to their gods continued, the most incredible event occurred – and this I swear is true! The large crystal on the lowest platform began to glow – bright red at first, then white-hot. The crystal then emitted a concentrated beam of blue light that shot straight at the cat and bird, striking them with a force that caused each to utter a loud cry – not a cry of pain, but more of an exclamation of ecstasy. In short order, what must have been their souls arose from each, briefly hovered above their bodies and then shot straight for their respective mummies on the platform below. A loud "swoosh" was audible as their diaphanous spirits flew downward. And as their life-forces entered their mummies, each bolted upright for an instant as if coming to life. The beam of light then ceased, and the crystal shattered into several large pieces, right before our very eyes. With this, the ceremony ended and Katt and Horus lay motionless; their souls drained from their animal bodies, but absorbed by their mummies. The prayers they intoned to their gods had been answered!

"*Sacre bleu, mon amis,*" shouted Homes, "we have witnessed a miracle! For contrary to conventional wisdom, we have encountered a bird that changed its feathers and a leopard that changed its spots. Will wonders never cease?"

We three hounds were mightily moved by what we witnessed that night, and agreed to take no action until the following day. The first item on our agenda the next morning was to proudly inform the Rab-Bits of the recovered mummies. And, as you might imagine, the good news caused me to endure not one, but two unwelcomed hugs from the overly elated hares!

Next, we met with the media and told the following half-true tale concerning our investigation:

Kitt E. Katt and Horus stole the mummies and hid them in a secret room beneath the museum. Their motive was to manufacture mummia — a drug made from ground mummy and used as an elixir of life. However, their first batch of tonic was far too potent and resulted in a lethal overdose. Arrangements for services and burial will be announced at a later time.

Yes, dear reader, we told a fib, but who would trust the truth? Do you believe my account, even though I swear it's fact? No, no you don't, for no one could believe that we saw two souls and their mummies reunite. So, here's my point: it was better to fudge the truth so the mummies of Katt and Horus will not be disturbed, again.

Last on the agenda was for Homes and I to review our adventure. I recall the day well, for our meetings with the Rab-Bits and the media caused a later-than-usual lunch; something that is always traumatic for me, since I love my food as much as life itself! The tardy mid-day meal was followed by our debriefing session. And I began the interview by asking Homes how she had deduced the involvement of Katt and Horus in this most implausible event.

"That's a good place to start, my dear Dr. Walk. Based on the hare's tale, I concluded that this caper was the work of someone on the museum staff, and that the mummies were still inside the building. Furthermore, I was certain that Kitt E. Katt and Horus were behind this mystery, for I gathered much incriminating evidence during our short visit with them."

"What? What? You found some evidence during our visit?" said I in surprise. "I sensed that Katt wanted rid of us in the worst way, Homes, but, otherwise, all I recall are those scrumptious chocolate chip cookies."

"Your never ending quest for food, doctor, distracted the cat and bird and allowed me to observe their office at will. So, once again, old boy, I could not have made the following connections without your aid."

"As you now know, doctor, Horus and Kitt E. Katt needed full control of the mummies to carryout their reunification ritual. To scare off the Rab-Bits, and thereby gain control, they devised an ingenious scheme to make the curses come true. If you'll recall, one curse warned that he who defiled the mummy would *'burn inside, suffer hair loss, and be cooked with the damned.'* During our time in Katt's office, I spied a vial of red powder which I secretly slipped into my cape. Later analysis revealed the substance to be cayenne pepper, a fiery herb that is tasteless to a hare, but one that causes a severe burning sensation as it passes through the digestive tract. Thus, it was just a matter of spiking the Rab-Bits' meals with red pepper to cause the burning innards promised by the curse."

"You are amazing, Homes, truly amazing!" gushed I. "But how did the hares lose their hair, old girl?"

"Interestingly enough, doctor, cayenne pepper also works as a powerful sedative when ingested by a hare. With the hares drugged into a deep sleep, the cat licked patches of fur from their bodies, furthering the illusion that their hair loss was due to the curse. Do you remember Kitt E. Katt grooming himself as we entered his office yesterday? He was ridding his body of recently-licked rabbit fur which I noticed lying at his feet. And speaking of fur, the clump of fur on the metal gurney was planted there by Katt and Horus to throw off investigators."

"Bravo, Homes! Magnificent detective work!" congratulated I, as I marveled at the genius of this special Corgi. "But what of the falcon shadow seen by the hares as they awoke from their naps? How did the shadow appear, and what was its purpose?"

"Ha, an easy answer, Dr. Walk, for I noticed a large flashlight under Katt's desk. Do you remember the first curse, old boy? It began, '**Death comes on wings...**' To reinforce the promise of that curse and to continue the scare tactics, a falcon shadow was produced as Katt shined a beam of light on Horus."

"There was one more piece of evidence in Katt's office that helped to solve this case, doctor. It was *The Book of the Dead*, a collection of ancient Egyptian ceremonial prayers – prayers that must be chanted in a precise manner and order if the deceased's spirit is to successfully crossover to the 'Other World.' After spying *The Book of the Dead,* I was further convinced that Kitt E. Katt and Horus desperately needed the mummies for some religious purpose. And once you provided the key to the cipher, I was most certain of my suspicions. By the way, Dr. Walk, *The Book of the Dead* contains most of the prayers Katt and Horus recited last night."

"It's overly generous of you, Homes, to credit my work on the cipher," said I, ever so humbly, for I knew it was really she who had broken the code. "But why was the secret message necessary, and why was it written in reverse?"

"Again, it is an easy explanation, dear doctor. Due to old age, Horus the parrot could barely speak, and hence found it easier to communicate through writing. But the mirrors dangling 'round him addled his brain, and caused him to see his surroundings as a mirrored image; that is, he viewed the world backwards. Hence, he wrote in reverse, for that is how he perceived his 'mirrored world.' Somewhere along the line, he and Katt hit on the idea that reverse-imagining worked as a cipher. Katt, who often assisted the Rab-Bits, confidently discarded the coded message in the laboratory waste basket, the place where Inspector Hunter discovered it."

"And speaking of Horus, it was fortunate for our investigation that you fed him a cookie, Dr. Walk. When we found a chocolate chip cookie in the secret room, I was positive the cat and bird had been there, for the cookie had been unmistakably nibbled – just as we watched Horus nibble the cookie in Mr. Katt's office."

"Incredible work, Homes, truly incredible! But what enables you to assemble unrelated facts into a logical whole?"

"Well, Dr. Walk, to make sense of the evidence, I often use a principal known as *Ockham's Razor*. William of Ockham, a medieval monk, proposed that one should accept as most likely the simplest explanation that accounts for all of the facts – an idea I usually apply to my investigations."

"Amazing, Homes! You are truly amazing!" praised I. "Now, would you please use Ockham's logic to explain last night's supernatural event, for I am still mystified by that inconceivable experience?"

"I must confess, dear doctor, that logic cannot solve every puzzle. However, when that is the case, I find the *WAG* method of reasoning to be quite useful."

Having said that, Homes began to weave an explanation for the remarkable incident we witnessed the previous night.

"My library research included Howard Carter's 1922 excavation of King Tut's tomb, whence I learned a little known fact: mummies identical to those in the West Chester collection – that is, a crocodile, a leopard, a serpent and a falcon — were also found in Tut's tomb. However, those mummies disappeared shortly thereafter, stolen and sold on the black market to a private collector, no doubt."

"Because of our recent adventure, doctor, I'm certain that the animal mummies found with Tut are now West Chester Museum's very own. If you'll recall, Horus the bird claimed that his soul had been wandering in search of his mummy for 85 years. If we subtract 85 years from the current year of 2007, it gives us 1922, the very same year that Carter discovered Tut's tomb – no mere coincidence, sir!"

"Furthermore, Dr. Walk, *The Book of the Dead* holds that a soul may be separated from its mummy if the tomb is violated," explained Homes. "Hence, it is my opinion that the souls of the leopard and the falcon were split from their mummies when Tut's tomb was disturbed by Carter. Needing a place to survive until they could learn the secrets of reuniting with their mummies, those severed souls inhabited the bodies of numerous animals over the years, ending with the parrot and the cat."

"A most logical rationale on your part, Homes!" lauded I. "But why was a falcon feather discovered in the exam room? I would have expected a parrot feather, instead, old girl!"

"According to the *Book of the Dead*, Dr. Walk, to reunite a soul with its mummy takes an assortment of prayers over a period of several days. As the steps in the ceremony are completed, the petitioner – the bird and the cat, in this case – gradually takes on the appearance of the soul who inhabits it. Hence the parrot, whose body was inhabited by the soul of Horus the falcon, dropped a falcon feather as he and Katt stole the mummies. And speaking of Mr. Katt, his transformation must have been nearly complete, for he looked like a miniature leopard, did he not, sir?"

"Astonishing, Hannah, truly astonishing!" exclaimed I. "But I must confess that I don't understand why it took the souls of the leopard and falcon 85 years to reunite with their mummies. After all, Horus and Kitt E. Katt knew where the mummies were long before coming to West Chester. Why did it take them until now to perform the reunification ceremony?"

Before answering my question, Homes licked a forepaw and rubbed it across her white chest – an unconscious move she makes when enjoying a Q. & A. debriefing.

"The souls of Katt and Horus were held in limbo for 85 years simply because they lacked one essential prayer for reunification. The missing prayer was only recently discovered by chance when the Rab-Bits – with the aid of Mr. Katt – unwrapped the falcon mummy. With the required spell now located, Katt and Horus realized that reunification could proceed to a successful conclusion. And none too soon for the bird, Dr. Walk, for he claimed in the secret message that it was his *'last chance,'* since he was *'fading fast.'*"

"At any rate, the parrot and cat drugged the Rab-Bits with red pepper, stole the prayer and the mummies and moved them to the secret room for the reunification ceremony. However, in their haste, they dropped the crucial prayer along the way. Inspector Hunter discovered the prayer before Katt and Horus could find it, and gave it to Mr. Rab-Bit. Once Horus and Katt learned that Rab-Bit possessed the magic words, again, they drugged the hares so they could steal the incantation – something they were in the act of doing at the very time we visited the museum yesterday."

I pulled another cold lamb chop from the dining table, devoured it in no time at all and then said to Homes, "Hannah, your powers of deductive reasoning never cease to amaze me, but I am still baffled by one small piece of this adventure. Just seconds before Mr. Rab-Bit bounded onto our veranda a few days back, you magically foretold that a rabbit with long, floppy ears was about to enter our lives. How on earth could you predict such an improbable event?"

Hannah snatched up her newest chew toy, a squeaky hedge hog, and tossed it about. Then she rolled onto her back and pumped her paws into the air as if pedaling a bicycle – something she does when greatly amused. Finished with her peculiar display of laughter, she answered my question.

"Why, it's elementary, my dear Doctor Walk. Due to my superior hearing ability, I detected the distinctive footfalls of a hare hopping up the sidewalk and onto our stairs. Having read the news article of the missing mummies, I presumed it was Rab-Bit who had come to request our assistance. Turns out I was correct, eh, Sprouty, old boy?"

"Bravo, Hannah!" exclaimed I. "But I fail to see how you knew the hare had long, floppy ears."

"Well, dear doctor, I sometimes reason like most folks do. I use the *WAG* method."

"Yes, yes, the *WAG* method, Homes," replied I, puzzled that I hadn't heard of this form of disciplined thought before now. "You mentioned it earlier, old girl. What exactly is this *WAG* method?"

"Well, Dr. Walk, lacking the facts to form a logical conclusion, and that's most folks most of the time, they use the most convenient form of thought – a process commonly known as the *Wild Ass Guess!*"

After another hearty laugh – from both of us this time – I paid Hannah Walk Homes my highest compliment.

"Homes, your ability to think logically has reached sheer perfection, sheer perfection, I say!"

Homes sat on her haunches and pointed her right forepaw at me – a posture she often assumes when about to make a profound statement.

"Sprouty, old friend," began Hannah in the humblest of voices, "I thank you for your words of adulation, but we mustn't lose sight of two realities. To begin with, it's quite evident that you and I make a good team, for I could not have solved this mystery without your help. Secondly, my good dog, we must always remember the primary principle passed down from the Renaissance masters."

"And what significant belief would that be, Homes?"

"Why, it's elementary, my dear Dr. Walk! Those artistic giants comprehended excellence, and hence appreciated this ultimate truth:

Only God is perfect!

Stenographers Note: According to Dr. Walk, the Rab-Bits soon recovered their health, their hair and their good names. They also resumed their duties of museum curators, and preside over the mummies of Katt and Horus to this very day. The good doctor finished his update with these noble words: "Homes may well chastise me for another mutilated maxim, but, as I always say, *let sleeping mummies lie.* May the souls of the bird and cat rest in peace for eternity!"

Some tales are make-believe and some tales have actually happened. You can rest assured, dear reader, that everything in this tale is true — whether it happened or not.

ABOUT THE AUTHOR, ARTISTS AND STORIES

Clint Heverly, a retired teacher, taught in the public and private schools of northern Delaware for over 30 years. He currently resides in Harrisburg, PA with his best friend, editor and wife, Kathleen. You can reach Clint at: HEV1998@AOL.COM.

Liz Walk, artist of the companion portrait, *Franklin Heverly: Leader of the Pack,* is the author's niece. She lives in San Diego, CA with her husband, Christopher, and pup, Hannah – the model for "Hannah Homes."

Denise Eileen Thurman, artist of the companion paintings *Rules for Big Dogs* and *The Curious Case of the Hairless Hare*, is the author's niece. She lives near Sonoma, CA with her inspirations; husband, Ryan; daughter, Naomi Rose; and orange kitty, Jasper Marmalade.

Connie Coyne painted the portrait referenced in *The Tale of the Lost Dogs.* She lives on Hilton Head Island, SC. You can visit Connie's work at: www.portraitsbyconcetta.com.

John W. Grover of San Diego did the cover photo titled "Dog Squad." His work is copyrighted, and all rights are reserved.

Every Dog Has His Day was written for the author's brother, John. All dogs named in the tale have been a member of John's pack at some point in time. Franklin still refuses to pull the sled, and the sled dogs actually bay like a pack of wolves — an amazing spectacle to behold.

Rules for Big Dogs was written for Clint's sister-in-law, Bernadette Henning, and the dogs that have been in her life — Fritz, Ivan, Josh and Kingston.

The Tale of the Lost Dogs was written for the author's good friends, Susan Van Arsdale and Albert Kinal. Their pup, Marley, wanted them to understand how she mysteriously arrived at the animal shelter, and why she's so afraid of large trucks, loud noises and confined spaces.

The Curious Case of the Hairless Hare was written for Elizabeth Walk. May the souls of Hannah and Sprouty live in Lizzie's heart for ever and ever.

8184715R0

Made in the USA
Charleston, SC
18 May 2011